Pridi

Village Affairs

THE RULE OF THREE

KRISTIAN PARKER

To Connie

Don't skip the good bits

The Rule of Three
ISBN # 978-1-80250-963-2
©Copyright Kristian Parker 2022
Cover Art by Kelly Martin ©Copyright June 2022
Interior text design by Claire Siemaszkiewicz
Pride Publishing

Published in 2022 by Pride Publishing, United Kingdom.

Pride Publishing is an imprint of Totally Entwined Group Limited.

THE RULE OF THREE

Dedication

This is for the Amazing Gays! My life took a turn when I met you all, and I love it.

Chapter One

Disco music blasted from the float passing by, and the crowds jamming the pavements dancing and waving in the spring sunshine cheered as a drag queen belted out *Holding Out For A Hero* at the top of her lungs.

A six-foot-tall man dressed as Wonder Woman threw a condom directly at Ed Cropper It ricocheted off his head and fell straight into his beer.

"Lo siento," 'she' cried and blew him a kiss.

She disappeared into the crowd, soon to be replaced by a marching band in stockings and suspenders. The parade waited for no one.

Ed fished the rogue item out of his beer and slid it into his shirt pocket.

James Durkin wrapped his arm around his shoulder. "Could you be any more Yorkshire? Waste not, want not?" he asked, laughing.

Ed leant into the hug, the throng of sweaty bodies pushing them together and the overwhelming smell of poppers permeating through the crowd. It only ever gave him a headache. He wondered what the hell anyone was doing sniffing them in the glaring Spanish sun.

"*Ah, guapo, guapo,*" shouted another drag queen, resplendent as Ursula from *The Little Mermaid*. She made a beeline for Ed and James, kissing them both on the cheeks before plunging their faces into her bosom.

They gasped as they came up for air and she blew kisses.

"It's bloody *mental* this year." James grinned.

The parade tailed off, leaving the crowd to disperse. Every bar had rainbow flags and cheap shots, but several years' experience had taught Ed that Maspalomas Pride was a marathon, not a sprint...although the glint in James' eye said he'd happily hit the booze.

"Right. Come on, you," Ed said. "Let's get some supplies and have a disco nap. Keep your strength up."

"Spoilsport," James replied.

They broke off from the crowd and wandered down an alley towards the apartment they'd rented. It was so close to everything that they'd snapped it up the second they'd come home last year.

James put his shirt on and walked with a spring in his step. Ed caught sight of them both in a boutique window. The drag queen had been right. They did make a handsome couple. Six-foot-three James had piercing blue eyes, a receding hairline that he shaved and lightly tan skin. Ed, on the other hand, had long dark curls, a beard and an even deeper tan from working outdoors most of his life.

Once inside, the cool relief in the supermarket made Ed gasp. It had been so hot in the middle of that crowd. James stood by the huge fan, letting his shirt billow behind him.

"What are you like?" Ed chuckled, picking up a basket and starting to think about what they needed.

James followed him up the aisle. Ed picked up some juice and bits to snack on. He absolutely refused to turn the cooker on in the apartment, but they had to survive, didn't they? He turned and saw James holding up eggs, bread and cheese.

"Please can I have your French toast for breakfast?" James asked with his pathetic puppy-dog face.

Ed sighed. "Not a chance, buster. You can take me out for French toast."

James slowly dropped the items in the basket. "But no one makes it like you do. You're the best French toast chef this side of Paris."

Ed couldn't resist those eyes. "Fine, seeing as it's you."

"Thank you, Eduardo," James said with a wink. "I'll make it worth your while."

It made Ed cross when James called him that and he bloody knew it. "Will you now?"

"Definitely."

"Then you've definitely got a deal."

Ed went to kiss him but leapt like a scalded cat as James put a hand on his chest and pushed him away.

"What are you doing?" James whispered, checking around the deserted aisle to see if anyone had seen them.

Ed's chest still stung from where James' fingertips had rejected him. "Nothing." He continued walking up the aisle but could sense James wasn't following him and spun round. James had that confused face he used to pull in primary school when asked a particularly difficult question. Ed had found it adorable then and he still did.

"What is the matter with you?" James asked calmly.

It drove Ed mad that he never seemed to lose his cool. Ed threw the basket down on the floor with a clatter. "Ten minutes ago, you were happy to kiss a drag queen and take your shirt off. Now you push me away?"

James snatched up the basket. "Are we having an argument in the fucking shampoo aisle?"

"No, James. We couldn't do that because someone might hear us," Ed replied and stormed past him and out of the shop.

Tears were threatening to escape as he dashed across the busy street and down another alley which led to their apartment. He had the key and let himself into the dusty stairway where they'd kissed on nearly every step after they'd got home the night before.

Today he stomped up each one, desperately trying to leave his anger on them but only feeling more uptight the higher he climbed. By the time he got inside, the tears had gone and he paced the apartment. James would be here any minute and Ed really didn't want to ruin the holiday by having a row.

He grabbed a beer from the fridge and walked out onto the balcony. The dull thud of the dance music from the huge party a stone's throw away swept across the rooftops. Gaggles of men would be dancing in each other's arms. Not afraid of anything.

Ed had always known he was attracted to men, but there had only ever been one he'd truly wanted. The man charging across the street below with a bag of shopping. He took a long slug of the cold beer and waited for the intercom to sound. It didn't take long before the harsh buzz filled the room. With a sigh, he wandered over.

"Are you going to let me in?" James' crackly voice questioned him.

Ed pushed the button and replaced the receiver. As a couple, they weren't the type to be constantly arguing and making up. They achieved this mainly as Ed did everything he could to keep the peace. He hated confrontation. It upset him and he'd replay it over and over, long after James had forgotten about it.

But he'd started this one and now James' footsteps echoed on the stairs. He would soon be wanting answers and Ed just wasn't ready to have the conversation he'd been practising for a while now. He went out onto the balcony again. James had a habit of filling a room and could be totally overpowering. Ed had always been more the type to shrink and marvel at how James could find a way to talk to anyone.

James came through the wooden panelled door and threw the shopping bag down onto the glass dining table. "Are you going to talk to me?" he asked, joining Ed on the balcony. He took his beer from his hand and had a swig.

Ed got up and padded inside. James' eyes bored into him as he got another drink from the buzzing fridge. It annoyed him that James had left the door open. He worried about mosquitos getting in, but the look on James' face hadn't lessened any and he thought it best to leave it for now.

"I'm still waiting, Ed."

Ed went back outside and sat on the rickety old chair. "Why couldn't you kiss me?" he asked eventually.

"You know why," James said, leaning against the railing. "What if someone sees us?"

Ed threw his hands up in the air. "We're miles away from anyone we know. And who cares if they do?"

"It's just not my thing. You know it isn't."

But what if it's mine? Ed couldn't face carrying on this conversation. They had dinner plans for the evening and he had no intention of eating with a cloud hanging over them. "Fine, whatever. I'm sorry I caused a scene. It just hurt me, you know?"

He got up to put the shopping away. James grabbed hold of his arm and drew him inward, wrapping his arms around his shoulders. Ed could smell the citrussy aftershave James had bought at the airport. It worked well on him, and he allowed himself to be drawn into a hug.

"You daft bugger. I love you no matter what. I wouldn't do anything to hurt you and I'd bloody kill anyone who did."

Feeling the strong arms resting on his shoulders made everything all right again. It always had.

"Come here," James said with a glint in his eye.

He moved Ed so he faced out to the whole of Maspalomas and stood behind him, lifting his arms like Leo did to Kate in *Titanic*.

"I bloody love this man," James shouted, almost deafening Ed in the process. "I always have and I always will."

A few people down below cheered. James spun him around and planted his lips on his. "There you go. Happy now?"

With that, he went inside and busied himself putting the shopping away. Ed watched him, marvelling at how pleased with himself James seemed. But the nagging doubt inside Ed still gnawed away at him. James had done it to keep him sweet, not because he wanted to. This secret love affair seemed to be all James wanted. A week in the sunshine every year then sneaking around the village they lived in for the rest of it.

Ed sighed and tried to shake the feeling that had been creeping into his mind for months.

The feeling that this...wasn't enough for him anymore.

Chapter Two

A week later and the clouds that gathered over the little Yorkshire village were dark and threatening, but the stone-built houses that had stood for nearly two hundred years had weathered worse storms and rain than this. Napthwaite's cluster of cottages huddled around a green and were flanked by the pub and the church — temptation and salvation in one handy location.

James peered out of the window of The King's Arms at the oncoming gloom. Almost on cue, the church bells chimed to let him know it was two o'clock.

"You're going out in that?" Becky, his regular barmaid, said.

"I won't melt," he replied.

James turned and took in the pub, his kingdom. The low beams of the ceiling, where many a tourist banged their head, felt as though they gave him protection, and the wobbly walls that came with an old property wrapped around him. He knew every picture of the local landscapes on the walls and every brass ornament that filled the shelves. He'd had to polish them enough times as a kid to get his pocket money.

Becky cleared the table next to him. "Another, Bill?" she asked old Bill, the only customer in the place.

James hated weekdays. He shouldn't really have Becky working, but he had other plans for the afternoon. He followed her behind the bar where she started to pull Bill's pint. "I'll only be a couple of hours. Will you be okay?"

He'd known Becky since her mother had been the barmaid here, and when she'd retired to travel the canal ways with an artist lover she'd picked up in Majorca, it had made sense to employ twenty-year-old Becky. That had been two years ago, and he would be stuck without her, even if she had got far too cheeky for her own good.

She glanced at Bill in the corner. He could make a pint last an hour, especially in the winter when the fire roared and the wind hammered at the windows. James didn't mind. Bill lived with his wife, Betty, and their seven cats, so James couldn't begrudge him a bit of me time. Even if he did leave cat hair all over the furniture.

"I think I'll cope," Becky said.

"Put one in the pump for Bill. I'm feeling generous," James said with a grin at how Bill suddenly perked up. "Right, here I go."

He scurried through the kitchen at the rear of the building. *Hardly a kitchen really.* When his mother had ruled the roost, she had produced some of the finest bar meals in the area. Nowadays they either reheated or deep-fried things from the freezer. He really did mean to do something about that.

Big dollops of rain hit his bald head as he dashed across the car park to his black BMW X7. Ed had said he didn't need a penis extension, but he loved his pride and joy.

He fired her up with a wheel spin that even he blushed a little at and set off. Even a sleepy village like Napthwaite hadn't escaped expansion and a terraced Edwardian street of shops branched off from the green.

As he drove down Queen Street, he waved at Liz scrubbing the windows of her mini supermarket. His sister, the dynamo. She couldn't sit still for five minutes. She would want to know why he'd abandoned his post at this time of day.

The in-car system told him he'd received a text before he'd even passed the village hall which bookended Queen Street, standing guard as the last building before Knott Wood.

What are you up to?

Liz. Right on cue. She would have to wait.

Ed's farm sat about a mile out of the village and, really, he could have walked, but he'd only had his car six weeks and needed any excuse to take her out for a spin. She bounced up the farm track and he winced at every pothole that threatened his bodywork. He made yet another mental note to nag Ed to get this fixed. He would need a tank to get up here soon.

He pulled into the yard and parked next to Ed's Land Rover. They had spent hours here as kids. The stone barn and cow shed had housed so many dens they'd made out of bales of hay. Ed's dad had never minded them playing as long as they were careful and didn't scare the cows. Ed's mum would have something delicious baking and, in the summer, she would open the top part of the stout white farmhouse's stable door so the smells would entice them in.

The rain had started to really come down now. James scrabbled in the backseat for the bottle of wine he'd taken from behind the bar. He frowned when he saw a half-eaten tennis ball rolling around on the floor of the car, and grabbed that too.

He let himself into the warm kitchen, dripping onto the slate flagstone floor. Ed leapt up from his old leather chair by the fire.

"You're soaked," he said, coming over.

"Well, it's raining. Hadn't you noticed?"

Ed took the bottle of wine he held out and made room for it on the cluttered kitchen worktop. James wished he would ask Mrs Chan from the village to clean for him. She worked wonders at the pub. He knew times weren't great for farmers, but Ed could afford it. The faded yellow of the kitchen cupboards could use a lick of paint too.

"Funny man," Ed said. "I was up in the paddock at six this morning, thank you."

James kissed him. "Eduardo, my macho man."

Ed scooted out of his grasp. "Oh no, I don't want a soggy cuddle. You'll have to get out of those."

James threw the tennis ball down to Madge who lay on her bed by the fire. She received it grumpily and set to work chewing away.

"Yours, I believe."

Ed removed James' coat and started to unbutton his shirt. He put them over two of the mismatched chairs that surrounded the oblong wooden dining table, then, with a wink, started to pull at James' belt, flicking the button on his trousers and letting them fall to the floor. He ran his hands over James' body, resting on the waistband of his boxers.

"I don't think the rain got to them," James said.

"Better to be safe than sorry."

James kicked his shoes and socks off before pulling his boxers down. He stood naked in front of Ed.

"I have a suspicion you have designs on me, Ed Cropper."

Ed knelt and picked up his trousers. He licked the end of James' hard cock.

"Whatever gave you that idea?" Ed stood and put the trousers over the chair nearest to the fire. "Go on upstairs. I'll hang these properly for you."

"You might as well hang yours up while you're at it." James smiled.

"They're not wet."

"No, but you look better out of them."

James slapped him on the arse and walked up the creaky stairs to Ed's room. He sank down on the old iron bedstead that squeaked at his weight. Ed had lit candles and they threw shapes on the uneven white stone walls. It had been a hard week and he had missed Ed.

He absentmindedly stroked his cock as he listened to Ed busying himself downstairs. It twitched as he heard another creak on the stairs.

Ed came into the room naked and holding two glasses of wine.

"I meant that for you tonight." James laughed. "Drinking in the afternoon? You'll get me fired."

Ed crawled onto the bed and kissed his neck then handed him a glass.

"One won't hurt."

James took a sip. It tasted of oak and blackberries. He'd selected it himself after a boozy weekend at a vineyard in France. "Remember the night we discovered this?" he asked.

Ed straddled him and leant in for a kiss, letting James taste the wine on his lips. "I should do. I could barely walk the next day."

James put his glass down on the chair that doubled as a bedside table and ran his hands down Ed's body. His cock had sprung into life feeling Ed's resting on it. Their Spanish holiday seemed a lifetime ago.

Ed put his glass next to James' and kissed him. In a second James spun him over and lay on top of him. Ed curled his legs around James' waist, his hands travelling down his arse cheeks.

James ran his hands through Ed's dark curls. Pulling up for air, he kissed Ed's neck, smelling his woody aroma. He knew where his sweet spots were and Ed squirmed.

"I've missed you," Ed murmured, but James silenced him with another hungry kiss.

He moved his way down Ed's body, a body he knew almost as well as his own but that he craved every day. He planted kisses on Ed's hard stomach. He made him squirm as he bit his protruding hip bone. Then, farther down, he took Ed's cock into his mouth. Ed started to move his hips in time with James' lips.

Ed writhed as James bobbed his head up and down, taking him in, then almost releasing him. Ed pulled James' head up, leaning forward to kiss him. He shuffled forward so his legs wrapped James' waist. James supported him and they never broke their kiss.

Ed moved away, onto all fours. "You know what I want."

James had a fair idea. He dove his tongue into Ed's arse. Ed buried his groan in the pillow. James revelled in those noises and worked Ed's arse, first with his tongue, next with his fingers. He licked the salty pre-cum off Ed's cock as he worked his fingers inside his channel. When he could wait no more, he grabbed the lube from the top of the chair and covered his throbbing cock and Ed's hole with it.

Holding Ed by the waist, he pushed the tip of his cock against him. Ed took hold of his hands. James felt resistance, then slowly slid inside, Ed digging his nails into James' fingers.

"Oh God, I need you," James murmured.

"Show me how much," Ed retorted.

James moved his hips. Ed moaned and dropped his head. James knew this sign to carry on. To give him more. He picked up the pace. The old bedstead that had played witness to many afternoons like this creaked as he fucked him.

He pounded at Ed's hole.

He loved to see Ed's face when he fucked him so turned him around. Grabbing both of Ed's ankles, he spread Ed's legs and guided his cock back inside.

"Yes, James," Ed moaned.

Ed looked so sexy, his legs wide, James' cock diving in and out. Ed tugged at his own cock.

"I'm going to come," James panted.

James' orgasm exploded in Ed. Every drop left his heart almost bursting out of his chest. Ed came a second later, his feet resting on James' shoulders. He arched his hips and cried out.

James fell forward and took Ed in his arms.

"You'll get this everywhere," Ed shouted, trying to wriggle free.

James rubbed the cum into his stomach. "Then we can have a shower together, can't we?"

Ed gave in to the arms wrapping around him and snuggled against James' chest. "That sounds like a good plan."

They lay there for a while, their bodies entwined.

"Gran Canaria seems like a lifetime ago, doesn't it?" Ed said, running his hand across James' chest.

"Yeah. The bloody real world came knocking."

James took hold of his hand, entwining his fingers in Ed's.

"It wouldn't have to," Ed said tentatively.

A flash of anger ran through James. "Don't start. We're having a nice afternoon."

Ed shifted onto his front. "Start what? Don't you want us to be together properly?"

James couldn't understand why Ed would want to spoil their time together when he'd gone to so much trouble. Then it struck him. The whole thing had been planned. He pushed Ed away and got off the bed.

"Where are you going?"

"For a shower."

Ed looked crestfallen. "I take it you won't want my company after all."

Guiltily, he sat on the bed and took Ed's hand. "It's not that I don't love you. You know I do. I can't face everyone knowing my business."

Ed squeezed his hand. "You're the only person in the world who compares yourself to him, you know."

Suddenly the room felt small. "I can't just announce to the world that I'm gay. I've got the pub and the parish council and rugby. God knows what Liz would make of it. It's different for me."

Ed pulled his hand free. "Different than poor lonely old Ed. Is that what you're saying?"

James ran his hand through his hair. He wanted to stay calm and talk this through, but Ed wasn't being reasonable.

"That's not what I'm saying."

"We wouldn't have to live together or rub it in people's faces. James, we're both thirty-two. We're not kids playing around. Don't you think about the future?"

"It will never happen, Ed. You can try to manipulate me with wine and sex all you like. I've been clear with you."

Ed got off the bed and threw his bathrobe on. "James, we have to start talking about this seriously. I need to know that we have a future. You have to stop letting ghosts rule your life or there's no point to this."

James wouldn't be cornered. "Are you serving me some kind of ultimatum?"

At first Ed seemed unsure, but then stared James in the eyes with certainty. "Yes, I think I am."

James' rage came from nowhere. "Then you lose, Ed. I won't be pressured into doing something I don't want to."

He barged past Ed and out of the door.

"Where are you going?"

"I'll get dressed downstairs. Don't follow me. I'm sorry I wasted your time all these years."

He stormed out of the room, letting the heavy wooden door bang behind him. He tried to drown out Ed's sobs as he banged down the stairs. His own tears didn't start until he got safely in his car.

Chapter Three

He strode up the lane, past the imposing gates to Thorpe Hall. He'd had to get out of the pub for an hour. He couldn't focus on anything. It had been a week since he'd stormed out of the farm and Ed had been silent. They had argued before, but usually one of them gave in. Usually Ed.

He stopped at the bridge before the green to take a break from the heat. He leant against the mossy stone and stared across at the pub that had been his whole life. He remembered his father treating it like another part of the family. They couldn't go on holiday when the other kids did because the pub needed all his attention. They never had days out together in the summer because he didn't dare leave.

The familiar lump appeared in James' throat when he thought about his parents. It had been a decade since they had gone and it still felt raw. Then his mind turned to Ed. He had no idea where this had come from. He had never mentioned them being open about who they were before. But he knew Ed bottled things up. The fact he never spoke about his own parents told James that.

The babbling stream rushed below him furiously. So much anguish must have happened in this village and still the water flowed. He stared up at Briar Woods on the hills that rose behind the church. They had guarded this little group of people for centuries. It made their problems seem so insignificant.

He had tried to contact Ed countless times, but it had gone to voicemail. He'd even driven up and banged on the door. Madge had greeted him with her usual bark which meant Ed was in there, but the door remained unanswered.

With a sigh he got up and carried on through the green, enjoying the shade the beech trees that lined the street gave him.

"Morning, James," Mrs Turnbull shouted as she vigorously pruned the rose bush in her front garden.

"Morning, Mrs T."

Her husband had been a great friend of his father. They'd used to go on golfing holidays together out of season. *Both gone now.*

On Queen Street, there were a few people popping in and out of the shops. Most of them waved at him and he returned their cheery greetings.

He needed to pick up some milk and would have to brave his sister. He'd tried to avoid her for the past week, no mean feat in a village like this. She could be relentless in her pursuit of the truth.

Luckily, she lived the busiest life in Napthwaite. She had taken over the shop from Mrs Brannigan about six years ago once Joel, her youngest, had started at school, turning it around from a pretty rubbish grocer's to a one-stop shop for most of the village. Well, one-stop if people weren't too fussy what they ate.

He wandered listlessly inside. Daylight meant nothing in Liz's treasure trove. She believed that windows took up good shelving space. Other than the front window — she would never get rid of that. Her cash register and bridge of this operation lay there. From this vantage point, she managed to see everything that went on.

Liz piled up cheap bottles of white wine on the front shelf where a neon sign declared *summer specials*. He frowned at the plonk. At least this place held no competition for The King's Arms.

She stood, surveyed her handiwork with a nod then barged past him. "Move out of the way." She almost shoved him into a display of breakfast cereal as she scuttled to her position by the window. She darted her head back and forth like a demented blackbird, trying to get a good view.

"What are you up to?" James asked.

She beckoned him closer. "That bloody Kathleen Brockbank has pushed me too far this time."

James rubbed his head. The feud with the newsagents across the road seemed to have been going on longer than time itself. "What's she done?"

His sister had been the beauty of the village, but hard times and harder work had taken its toll. Rapidly approaching her fortieth birthday, she looked ten years older.

"Don't say it like that," she said. "Like I've lost my marbles. She's stocking essentials now. Bread, milk, butter." She stood with her arms folded over her tabard, presenting evidence to an imaginary courtroom.

"What's the problem with that? Seems a good idea. They're open way later than you."

Liz angrily rearranged the packets of sweets she piled up near the tills to tempt whining kids. "That's exactly what she says at the same time as undercutting me. Snide bitch."

He couldn't face this. He trudged down the aisle of trifle sponges, beef paste and crackers that resembled cardboard. Would it kill her to stock something decent?

Grabbing four bottles of milk from the fridges, he steeled himself and walked up to the till.

"You wouldn't say the same if she started stocking booze," Liz said with a sniff, ringing the items up.

"Like you do, you mean?" James replied.

"He's got you there, Mum," said Dean, coming in from the storeroom with an armful of tins.

She huffed. "Less of your lip, first born. That'll be four pounds sixty, little brother."

Liz had made it very clear that family discount would not be part of her business plan. She also criticised every supermarket carrier bag she found in his house as disloyalty. James wondered if she honestly expected people to make meals from the tins of meat and pots of noodles she stocked.

He handed over a five-pound note. "Keep the change. Get yourself something nice."

She stared at him as if noticing him for the first time. "You're still in a mood, I see."

He started to pick up the milk. He wished Becky had come. Liz's incessant pecking took stronger fortitude than he had today.

"You've been like a bear with a sore head for the best part of a week now. What's the matter with you?"

"Nothing is the matter with me."

She started to absentmindedly dust the till. "Okay, man of mystery. I asked Ed the other day why you're being a grouch. He said you hadn't seen each other much lately. Don't tell me you got yourself a woman."

James started to pile up the bottles of milk in his arms. But Liz hadn't finished yet.

"Or perhaps Ed has got a woman and poor little James has been pushed out. Is that it? Lost your favourite playmate?"

He held the four bottles tight. "Or perhaps not everything is your bloody business, Liz. Now excuse me. I need some bread and I hear across the road's is cheaper and let's face it, yours is usually stale."

"Don't you even think about it, James Durkin. I'm warning you."

He barged out of the shop with her threats ringing in his ears. As he crossed the road, he knew she would be pressed up against the window. It served her right.

As he approached the enemy across the road, the door opened and out came Ed. They ran straight into each other, knocking James' milk to the road. One bottle burst open and instantly little rivers of white appeared in the cobbles.

"Oh, shit," Ed exclaimed.

"Don't worry about it," James mumbled, bending down to pick up the three still intact bottles.

"I'll give you some money for it."

James straightened up and looked deep into Ed's eyes. "Is that where we are now? Awkwardly giving me a quid for some fucking milk?"

He instantly regretted his outburst as Ed stood silent.

"How have you been?" James said, a little more gently.

"Awful. You?"

"Worse."

He had so many things he wanted to say, but they stuck in his throat. The newsagent's door opened again and Jenny Holdsworth came out.

"Hello, both," she said pleasantly as she headed off towards the green. "Oh, James. Rob said not to forget training is Wednesday this week, not Tuesday."

James nodded, and they watched her walk towards the green. "Well, I'd best be getting on. I've left Becky on her own." They started to walk their separate ways before he turned. "Ed?"

Ed turned. The eagerness on his face broke James' heart.

"Can't we find a way through this?"

James' heart felt as hopeful as Ed's eyes. He wanted things to be normal so desperately he could almost taste it.

"Have you changed your mind?"

"You know how I feel," James replied.

Ed came closer. "Which means we have no future. Not as friends or…anything else."

"Do you think your mum and dad would want you telling all and sundry our business?"

Ed's face turned to pure rage. James knew he'd stepped out of line. "Don't you bring them into this. Don't you dare."

"I didn't mean…"

"You know what? Take care of yourself, James."

Ed hurried away, not looking back even though James watched him until he disappeared into the Post Office. His gaze shifted to Liz's shop. She stood in the doorway, holding up a bottle of milk. He put on a brave face as he crossed over the street, tiptoeing around the puddles they had created.

"Thanks."

"On the house, little brother. Sorry I shouted at you."

Typical Liz. A storm would explode out of nowhere then she would survey the damage, full of remorse. She had been the same when they were kids. Their mother would make her have time out in the car park, by the stream, to think about the words she had used.

"I wouldn't really have bought bread in there," James said, taking the bottle from her.

"You bloody would, you pig-headed little shit," she replied, with a smile.

"Well, only to teach you a lesson."

Liz rubbed his arm. "I don't know what's gone on with you two, but I'm sure you'll sort it out. You've been best friends for nearly thirty years. Why don't you come for your tea tonight? It's your night off, isn't it?"

Mondays were his night off. He and Ed had called them movie nights and taken it in turn to choose what to eat and what to watch. Perhaps a night with the family would be perfect to take his mind off things. "Sure, I'll see you at six?"

"I'll make your favourite." She gave him a kiss on the cheek and went into the shop. She wasn't such a bad sister. Some of the time.

As he set off for to the pub, he cast a glance down the street and saw Ed walking towards his farm. The tears started to well up inside him and he dashed across the green.

Chapter Four

The cab pulled up on the green and Arthur Whittaker got out. His blond curls danced in the breeze and he brushed them out of his eyes. The car drove off and he took in his surroundings. If someone had drawn a typical Yorkshire village, they wouldn't have been far wrong with this place. He thanked his lucky stars he'd chosen to dress down in jeans and a T-shirt. Perhaps this place wasn't quite ready for his skin-tight white vest and incredibly short shorts.

Up to the left of the church was what must be the school where he had his interview in the morning. The church clock struck six, making him jump. It had taken three hours to get here from Blackpool, but it could be another planet. After the events of recent months, it was exactly what he needed.

"Hello, Mr Johnstone."

Arthur spun around to see an older lady in her garden attending to a very impressive rosebush. The gentleman she had called over stopped to chat, but they both noticed him at the same time.

He smiled cheerily but only got two suspicious stony faces in return. No doubt everyone would know everyone else's business here. He wouldn't have to get involved in that if he didn't want to.

After six failed interviews, his choices were pretty limited. This last roll of the dice would have to be the winner. He picked up his bag and marched inside the pub, almost banging his head on the low eaves as he came in. That familiar smell of old beer and chips greeted him. The place seemed to be deserted so no one saw his less-than-graceful entrance.

"Hello?" he called.

He heard movement in the back and a man came out, still chewing and wiping his mouth with a napkin. A ridiculously handsome man with close-cropped hair and a tight shirt that showed off a body he definitely worked on.

"Hi. Erm…Arthur Whittaker. I booked a room?"

The man looked him up and down. Arthur felt self-conscious with his small frame and skinny body in comparison.

"Ah yes, one night. Sorry, not quite with it today."

The handsome barman came around the side of the bar and held out his hand. "James Durkin. Pleased to meet you."

His strong handshake almost knocked Arthur off balance. He tried to match it but knew he'd failed miserably.

"If you could sign in over here and let me have a credit card? Just in case you try to do a runner," James said, raising his eyebrows.

Arthur followed him over to the cash register and picked up the registration form.

"Can I get you a drink?" James asked.

Arthur decided one wouldn't hurt even though he had every intention of spending the evening preparing for his interview and getting an early night. "Go on, then. I'll have a gin and tonic."

"You know what? I think I'll join you," James replied.

He busied himself getting the drinks. Arthur could barely concentrate on the task in hand as he cast furtive glances at James bending for the tonics and reaching up to the optics. *Oh yes, there's a body under there all right.*

By the time James presented the drinks, Arthur had finished the form and held out his credit card.

He raised his glass. "Cheers."

"What shall we drink to?" Arthur asked.

"Oh, how about that it's Tuesday?" James proposed.

"Here's to Tuesdays," Arthur replied. The gin tasted great. There were hints of orange and lime making it so refreshing. "That's amazing."

James seemed proud. "One of my old schoolfriends makes it. A couple of villages back the way you probably came. It's great, isn't it?"

Arthur realised he had the perfect candidate in front of him to find out a bit more about the village. He thought it best to remain a man of mystery.

"What brings you to Napthwaite?" James asked. He'd got the interrogation started before Arthur could even try. So much for the subtle approach.

"I've got an appointment nearby, tomorrow morning. I didn't want to leave it to chance so thought I'd better book a night. This place seemed the best around by far."

James seemed proud as he took a sip of his drink.

"It must be great to work here," Arthur continued.

The smile dropped from James' face. "Work here? I own it."

Arthur knew he would be blushing. "Oh, I didn't realise. I'm sorry. You look too young."

James threw his head back and laughed. A loud, booming laugh that almost made the brass ornaments clatter. "Now that is the most perfect digging yourself out of a hole I've ever seen."

Arthur grinned along with him. "So, what's Napthwaite like? Have you lived here all your life?"

James came out from behind the bar and took a seat next to Arthur. "I don't like staff drinking behind the bar, so I have to set an example," he explained. "Napthwaite? It's pretty quiet, truth be told. We have the odd festival, usually started by yours truly. I'm the chair of the parish council, too. I love this village."

"Sounds like you're the king of Napthwaite to me," Arthur said, the gin already starting to loosen his lips. He had to remember he wasn't in Blackpool anymore. His brand of flirtation might not go down well with the burly landlord in front of him.

"Some people would say I think I am," James said with that ever-present wink that gave Arthur so many signals. But then again, it could be wishful thinking.

At that moment, three older men came in. James jumped off his bar stool and returned to his post. They were clearly locals, as he had easy banter with them. Arthur watched and drained his gin. The men got their drinks and went to sit in the corner.

This place definitely had a friendly vibe about it, plus a drop-dead gorgeous landlord in the local pub. Arthur hoped he didn't bomb at the interview tomorrow. He could see himself spending a few years here. After everything that had happened in the last few months, he needed some peace.

"Am I all right to go up?" he asked James, grabbing his bag.

James threw him a key. "First on the left. Breakfast is from seven. Are you eating tonight?"

"Be bloody careful," one of the three men said.

"This bugger could burn water," said another.

James scowled at them. "It's not that bad."

"I'm fine. I got some bits at the station," Arthur said, tapping his bag. He set off up the stairs to find his room. He hadn't held out much hope, but it had a comfy double bed and the view looked over the rear of the pub, past the stream and to thick woods. He flung the windows open and let the May air flood in.

He laid his healthy salad, falafel and snacks he had picked up at the station out on the desk. It didn't seem very inviting, but he had vowed to treat his body better. Well, except for the odd gin, of course.

His mobile rang. "Hi, Mum."

"Hello, love. You there then?"

"Yep, safe and sound."

The worry in his mother's voice gave him pangs of guilt.

"What is it like?"

"Oh, it's really pretty. I could do well here I think."

His mother didn't say anything.

"Mum?"

"I still don't like you being away from us. It's very soon."

He took a deep breath. He had to be patient. "I know but we've been through this. The farther I am away from them the better. I'll be fine, Mum. I'm twenty-six now."

"But you're still my baby."

"I'd better go. I want to go through all the information the agency sent me. Let's face it, I need this bloody job."

"Well good luck. Your father sends his love. Bye, love."

"Bye."

He put the mobile down and emptied his rucksack of all the papers and booklets he had already pored over countless times. "Right then," he said to himself. "Let's do this."

Five hours later and his eyes were aching. He'd read everything through twice and what he didn't know about Napthwaite and its school wasn't worth knowing.

He glanced at the clock. Just gone eleven. He stretched and rubbed his eyes. He needed to sleep now, but his mind whirred ten to the dozen. Perhaps a nightcap would help.

The upstairs of the pub lay quiet, although he'd heard some people going into adjacent rooms.

He padded down the stairs. Maybe he had missed last orders. *Do they do things differently in the country?*

James sat on a banquette by the fireplace, alone with his thoughts. "Is everything all right?" he said, sitting up.

"Yeah. I couldn't sleep, so I thought I'd find out what the chances are of getting another one of those gins."

James leapt to attention. "Your wish is my command. It's pretty sad drinking on my own anyway. Take a seat."

Arthur did as James busied around. Just wearing joggers and hoodie, Arthur suddenly felt very exposed. Especially with James taking him in again in that way he had earlier.

"If you're cold, there are some blankets under that bench," James said.

It might have been May, but the nights were still a bit chilly. Arthur reached under for a woollen blanket that he wrapped it around him. James put his drink down with a second for himself.

"That will warm you up," he said with a smile.

"Thank you. I didn't bring my wallet. Is it okay to put it on my room?"

"I can't sell out of hours, so it will have to be on the house."

"That's very kind of you." Arthur took a swig. "God, it's too good. I would be drunk all the time if I had this in arm's reach."

"How come you can't sleep?" James asked.

"The old brain has a lot of thoughts sometimes."

James took another sip of his drink. "Thoughts can be a pain in the arse, that's for sure."

Arthur couldn't disagree there. He didn't want to say he had an interview at the school the next day. This guy seemed to know everyone around here and if he told him something he shouldn't know, it could get awkward.

"Where did you say you come from?" James asked.

"Blackpool."

His face lit up. "Really? Had some good trips there as a kid."

Arthur pulled the blanket closer. "Most people did. It's not the same living there." He studied the face in front of him. James seemed more vulnerable now the customers had gone.

"I guess. Bit more lively than old Napthwaite."

The swirly floral-patterned carpet and the picture of a smiling couple above the bar couldn't be more removed from the chrome and disco bars Arthur usually went to. "A bit too lively."

"Sounds like you're speaking from experience."

He had no idea why he'd decided to open up to this man, but something inside him couldn't stop. Maybe the gin had been stronger than he'd realised. "Let's just say there's a lot of temptation in my town. I got into a bit of trouble with it all."

James stared at him intensely. "Drugs?"

Arthur nodded and looked down. He couldn't bear the judgement.

"Life never runs smooth. Not for any of us. It's nothing bad to admit you had a wobble," James continued.

To his horror tears pricked his eyes. "It's a long and sorry tale, but I had a few months away and got myself together. Now I'm after a new challenge."

"So, it's a job interview tomorrow, is it?"

Arthur realised he'd given away more than he wanted to. "I'm trying different things on for size. I want to turn a corner."

James stood. "How about I get us another gin and tell you all about what it's like to live in this part of the world?"

Arthur smiled. "That would be lovely."

Another drink turned into a few and by the time they crept up the staircase, they were both feeling no pain. James was so easy to talk to and had him in fits of laughter at his descriptions of the villagers.

"Be careful. That next one squeaks," James whispered, pointing to the middle stair. "The last thing I need are guests moaning."

Arthur stepped dramatically onto the step above, which caused them both to giggle.

"I bet you've snuck in many a time," he whispered to his host.

"Not since I was a teenager."

Arthur detected a flash of sadness over James' face, gone as soon as he'd realised. Once on the landing, James turned to him.

"I'll say goodnight then."

"Thank you for the drinks. I'll return to staring at the ceiling. I probably should have gone for a jog to tire my body out instead of boozing."

In the half-light James looked so handsome. Arthur had really enjoyed his company. He had an innocent quality when one got past the bluster and bravado.

"You could always come upstairs and tire your body out."

A bad idea on so many levels, but he'd been away for six months and had thrown himself into getting a new job. He deserved a bit of fun. "Sounds like a plan to me."

James opened a door that led up more stairs to a big split-level attic room almost as big as the whole pub. He went to turn the light on, but Arthur took his hand.

"No need."

The moon shone in through the massive windows at one end. Arthur didn't let go of his hand and entwined his fingers around James', pulling his hand down to the small of his back.

James kissed him. The months of struggling with temptation and realising he had a problem with drugs seemed to wash away as Arthur focused on this kiss. James seemed hesitant too. They were standing on the edge of the diving board and just needed that one gentle push to dive in. Arthur ran his other hand up to James' broad shoulders and drew him closer, intensifying the contact. Arthur flicked his tongue into James' mouth and his cock sprang to life.

They leapt off the board, pulling at each other's clothes. James' shirt fell first, followed by Arthur's T-shirt. He ran his hands over James' hard muscular chest. James grabbed him by the arse and wrapped his arms around him, the hairs on his chest tickling against his hairless one.

"Do you have a bed around here?" Arthur said, coming up for air.

James pointed to a ladder.

"A bunk bed?" Arthur asked with a frown.

"A split-level mezzanine bed area in the eaves, you cheeky get," James said, kissing him, "Now up that ladder."

Arthur scrambled up, closely followed by James who shed the rest of his clothes on the way. James crawled on the bed and wrapped his arms around Arthur. The heat of another person's body felt incredible, and he could have kissed him forever. He moved James onto his back and straddled him, leaning forward so his cock rested on James' chin. James licked the end. This guy had him turned on in so many ways. He gripped Arthur's butt cheeks and guided his cock in between his lips. Arthur cried out as he sucked hard. He reached behind him and took hold of James' dick, starting to massage.

They moved in tandem together until Arthur moved down James' body. He dove straight for his dick and James sighed as Arthur's mouth enveloped him.

"Oh God yes."

Arthur stopped and ran his own cock against James', gripping them both and gently pulling at them.

James started to get up to kiss him, but Arthur pushed him down.

"Enjoy," he said with a twinkle in his eye.

He worked just James' cock now, his pace quickening. He wanted to see this man come.

"Come with me," James begged.

Arthur took his own dick in his other hand, pulling furiously. Their eyes locked with hunger. James reached forward and ran his hand up Arthur's thigh, gripping his hip bone.

"Don't stop," James begged. "I'm going to—" His body tensed and he came hard, covering Arthur's hand. "Oh, Jesus," he cried out, the aftershocks rippling through his body.

Never ceasing pulling at his own cock, Arthur took hold of James' hand where it still rested on his hip and entwined their fingers together. He was close and couldn't take his eyes from James'.

"Show me," James whispered.

Leaning back, Arthur let go. The orgasm built and exploded out of him. Panting, he kissed James. "I wanted to do that since I walked in this place."

James laughed. "I have a few more tricks in my repertoire, you know."

"I'm sure you do, but I've got an appointment in the morning." Arthur crawled to the edge of the bed and started to climb down the ladder.

"You're not staying?" James asked, surprisingly needy.

"That would be lovely, but something tells me I'd have less chance of getting to sleep if I stayed here." As he collected his clothes, the light flicked on. James' face appeared at the edge of the sleeping area.

"Arthur, listen. No one knows. In the village. No one knows about me."

Arthur climbed a little way up the ladder to plant a kiss on James' gorgeous lips. "You do you, James."

He left the room and went to his own. He flopped down on the bed and started to giggle. It might not have been the best sex he'd ever had in his life, but he'd passed another milestone. Martin and everything that had happened lay firmly behind him.

* * * *

The next morning, he nearly slept in. The gin had left him a little fuzzy around the edges, but the hot shower had done him no end of good. He thought he should skip breakfast. He could get something at the station after his interview—it might make both of them uncomfortable if James had to serve him eggs and bacon.

With his bag over his shoulder, he made his way up the road to the small primary school next to the church, tiny compared to his last school, which had had three hundred pupils. He had read last night that this place had something like fifty.

His footsteps rang out in the deserted hallway of the school. He would have liked to have met some of the children, but when he'd applied, Mrs Carrington had told him she needed a teacher as quickly as possible. Her previous colleague had died unexpectedly, hence a half-term interview.

A reed-thin lady with a mass of grey curls and horn-rimmed glasses came through the doors behind him.

"Arthur Whittaker?"

She thrust her hand out, which Arthur took. She had a firm, enthusiastic handshake. "That's right."

"Christine Carrington. Come on in."

He followed her into the old building. He loved the smell of schools. She led them into an office with things piled high everywhere.

"Ignore this. Mrs Hopkirk, our secretary, has told me on pain of death that I have to tidy up before we open the doors again next week."

Glancing around, Arthur didn't much fancy her chances.

"I'm sorry it's such an early interview, but there has been a lot of interest."

Arthur's stomach sank.

Christine clearly picked up on this. "Now come on, faint heart never won fair maiden. Why don't you start by telling me all about yourself?"

Arthur shifted uncomfortably. He didn't know whether to be totally honest. "I taught at Palatine Primary for four years after leaving university…" He faltered.

Christine smiled kindly. "I find truth is the best policy, Mr Whittaker. If we are to work together, I'd insist on it."

He swallowed hard. "I got into a bit of trouble with my lifestyle. I promise you I never let it interfere with my work."

At the facility where he'd stayed, they had encouraged him to speak openly, but being in a circle with similar struggling people felt like a very different prospect compared to sitting here.

"Go on," she said.

"I had a difficult relationship. My ex was dependent on drugs when I met him, and I guess I just slipped into his ways. Things got a bit much and I went away to get over things." He put his head down. He knew he'd just ruined a perfectly good opportunity and anyone else in his position would have lied.

"And how are you feeling now?"

He didn't even dare hope. "So much better. I haven't touched anything since November or seen my ex."

Christine sat in her chair, resting her notes on her knee.

"I think you are a very brave young man. We're none of us perfect. Now, how about you tell me all about your working life?"

The next hour flew by. He and Christine got on like a house on fire.

Christine glanced at the clock. "Oh, my goodness we're nearly out of time. Is there anything you wanted to ask me?"

"No, I don't think so," Arthur said, wistfully. He appreciated her being charitable and not just getting rid of him the minute she heard about the last six months.

"Right then. Obviously, I can't make it official until the end of the day but, Mr Whittaker, I'd start thinking about what you're going to pack. I don't see why we can't give you a trial run for the rest of the year and talk about September at a later date."

"Do you mean...?" He couldn't believe it.

Christine clapped her hands together. "I certainly do. Our children will absolutely love you. You have about five days to sort yourself out and I have a day of pointless interviews ahead of me."

Arthur's mind started to whirr. "But I will need to get a house sorted and —"

"Nonsense. You will lodge with me. You can have my son's old room. He and his wife hardly ever visit anymore. They're too busy living the high life in London to bother with his old mum."

Arthur couldn't believe his luck. He walked out of the school building and stood in the yard, facing down to the village, where The King's Arms proudly overlooked the green.

That was when it struck him.

Perhaps it hadn't been the best move in the world to sleep with James last night...

Chapter Five

As far as first days went, it had been pretty good. He had a class of twenty who were all desperate to tell him how their previous teacher had died unexpectedly.

His classroom sat on the first floor. It did feel quite macabre as Christine hadn't had time to remove the work from the previous half-term, so he had literally stepped into a dead woman's shoes. Evidently, she had died a couple of months ago. Her heart had given way and Christine had found her body when she hadn't turned up for school.

For the last part of the afternoon, he had prepared a lesson on telling one another about where they came from. The class had told him all about Napthwaite, Thorpe Tarn where they liked to swim, Knott Wood where they played and the playing fields behind the school.

He held up a picture of Blackpool Tower. "Does anyone know where this is?"

A young girl stuck her hand up.

"Yes…Emily," he said. Learning the children's names had been a crash course.

"That's Blackpool."

"Well done." He smiled. "This is where I lived before I came to Napthwaite."

Silence descended on the classroom. He panicked for a second that he'd made a bad call telling them.

"You lived in Blackpool and you moved here?" Joel Poole said. The son of two local entrepreneurs, he seemed to rule the roost.

"That's right, Joel."

Joel turned to Kevin Chan next to him and they both shook their heads in dismay.

Before he had a chance to defend himself from this seemingly crazy idea, the school bell rang and the children burst into life.

"Slow down," Arthur shouted. "No one wins a prize for being first out of the door."

They lined up and Arthur led them out to the playground where a gaggle of mothers waited patiently. It might be almost June, but rainclouds were brewing over the hill.

A little hand took hold of his. "Come and say hello to my mum," Joel said, beaming up at him.

Arthur allowed himself to be led over to a woman with mousy blonde hair, wearing a tabard that was covered by a fleece.

"Mum, this is Mr Whittaker," Joel announced proudly.

Liz held her hand out, which Arthur took. "Ah, the new teacher. We're glad you could come at such short notice. Poor Mrs Wilkinson. What a terrible do. Lay there for hours apparently."

Arthur didn't feel comfortable discussing his predecessor in the school playground. "Well, it's nice to meet you, Mrs Poole. No doubt we'll see each other again."

"Call me Liz. Everyone does. How are you finding Napthwaite?"

"He used to live in Blackpool," Joel offered. He obviously couldn't figure out this strangest of life choices.

"Is that right? I'm sure Napthwaite is better," Liz countered. "Right, you, let's get to the shop. I've left Dean on his own and the rush for sweets will be incoming. Welcome to the village, Mr Whittaker."

Arthur set off into the school building with a spring in his step. The children had been pretty well behaved, and he just knew working with Christine would teach him a lot.

As if on cue, he bumped into her in the entrance hall.

"First day done." He sighed.

"They didn't make mincemeat of you then?" Christine said. "I know, I'll call into the butchers and get us two lovely steaks for dinner. We deserve it. It's so good to have you here. Managing all of the little terrors for two weeks was far too much for an old lass like me."

"Fine, but you must let me buy the wine. I'll call into Poole's."

Christine waved her hand. "Don't buy the vinegar they sell there. All the locals know to call in at The King's Arms. It's pricey, but it's worth it."

Arthur had been dreading going into the pub, but he thought he had better get it over with. "Got you. I'll clean up my classroom and wander down. Do you mind if I take some of the work down from the walls. It seems a bit strange, you know…"

"Of course. We will all miss Alice, but it's your room now."

Relieved, Arthur vowed to set to work tonight. Having a dead woman's projects and writing staring down at him wasn't the most comfortable start.

"I thought I might ask the children to paint something that reminded them of her. It's good for them to address any feelings they have."

Christine smiled. "I think that would be a wonderful idea."

Some of the children hadn't been particularly happy to see him and he wanted to work through this.

"I must go and catch Mrs Chan. I'll see you at home."

He took a lot longer than necessary to take things down and arrange equipment ready for the next day. He kept glancing out of the window at the pub. When he could put it off no longer, he threw on his coat and went to leave. Standing at the door, he surveyed the classroom. He had a good feeling about this place and vowed to make a decent impression. Only James lay in the way of all this.

With purpose, he walked down the road towards the green and retraced his steps of only a few days before. If only he'd been sensible that night and not ended up in bed with the bloody local landlord. He opened the door and, stooping to avoid the damned beams, walked into the pub.

James and a young girl were behind the bar, chatting. A couple were eating in the corner and three young lads played darts. James froze when he saw Arthur walk in.

"Go on…" the girl next to him said.

"What?"

"The punchline, go on…"

"Oh, it doesn't matter."

Arthur approached the bar.

"What can I get you?" the barmaid said.

James stepped forward. "It's okay, Becky. I can serve this gentleman. Why don't you go and get your break?"

Becky frowned. "I'm not due for another hour."

Arthur could see James starting to panic. "Fine, I'll take mine. I'll be in the car park. The squirrels have been shitting on the car again."

He stared pointedly at Arthur—who couldn't fail to pick up the hint—before walking out to what he presumed was the kitchen. Becky shook her head.

"Never work in a pub," she said with a laugh. "What can I get you?"

"I'd like a decent bottle of red, please. Actually, make that two. Let's live dangerously."

The girl beamed. "We have a Shiraz, a Tempranillo or a Pinot Noir?"

He thought about what Christine would like. It wasn't the depths of winter just yet. It didn't feel right to get a heavy one.

"Let's go for the Pinot."

She reached below her and picked up two bottles, which she wrapped in paper. Arthur looked around the bar. He had fond memories of getting to know James in here, but he had a feeling they were going to work against him very quickly.

Becky rang the totals up on the till. "Twenty-five, ninety-eight please."

Christine wasn't wrong when she said they were more expensive than Poole's Mini Mart. He tapped his card against the proffered machine. They had better be good. Once out on the green, he followed the building around and found James pacing in the car park. Arthur couldn't help but wondering how this man had managed to keep a secret on the scale of staying in the closet for over thirty years.

"Hello," Arthur said, approaching him.

James glanced around, evidently checking for eavesdroppers. "What the hell?"

Arthur held his hands up. "This is totally my fault. I should have told you my appointment was for a job interview at the school."

James pulled him away from the kitchen door, towards the wall that backed onto the stream.

"The fucking school? My nephew goes there."

Arthur frowned. "What's his name?"

"Joel Poole."

"Oh, he's a lovely lad. You must be proud."

This did not seem to help James who seemed as though he were about to blow a fuse. "You are totally out of order. You let me sleep with you when you knew you were moving here?"

Arthur felt some sympathy for him, but he wouldn't stand for a dressing-down from James about life choices.

"Firstly, I hadn't even had my interview at that point, and secondly, you only told me you were living in the closet after you'd put your cock in my mouth, if you remember." He leant against the wall. "Look, relax. I'm not going to tell anyone am I? I'm new around here and the last thing I want to do is get a reputation. You can trust me, James."

James whirled around. "I'd better be able to. You could ruin my whole fucking life and believe me, you wouldn't want to." He stormed past Arthur and through the door of the pub.

Arthur sighed. *Nice one, Arthur. So much for starting off strong.* Only time would be able to sort that one out and perhaps he would give the pub a miss for a while. Trying to put it out of his mind, he walked through the village towards Christine's cottage.

A few of the parents he had seen in the playground were running errands and waved at him. He had never known such a friendly place. He'd only been here a day. The road turned a corner and headed out to countryside. He had loved Christine's house as soon as he'd clapped eyes on it.

Once the blacksmiths by the beck, the cottage had dark stone that contrasted perfectly with the white wooden windows. A little garden ran along the water side. On the road they had a bridge which he imagined had seen many an assignation, hidden from the village by the woods on the other side.

He let himself in the little gate at the side of the house. There were still two old stables where the blacksmith would have done his work. Christine now filled them with garden furniture and, bizarrely, an old rotting boat.

Byron, Christine's cat, came to investigate. He hadn't been too pleased at a stranger moving in, but Arthur had been there a couple of days now. Christine had insisted he feed him both days to show he came in peace. There seemed to be a begrudging acceptance forming.

"Hello," Arthur said, reaching out to stroke him and being greeted with a hiss. "Oh, fine. Not quite ready for that then."

Christine had travelled extensively and her décor reflected it. The lounge was an explosion of colour and culture with African masks from Namibia jostling for space on the wall with a picture of Venice she had picked up at a flea market. He walked through to the kitchen where Christine chopped vegetables at an alarming rate.

"There you are. Two bottles? On a Monday? I hope you aren't going to be a bad influence, Mr Whittaker."

Arthur winked. "Who knows?"

"You pour us two glasses and go on out to the garden," Christine continued.

He wandered out through the conservatory. A big, round wooden table sat right by the stream's edge. He sat and took a big glug of wine. It had all been a bit of a whirlwind from being interviewed and coming here, but the lady at the agency had warned him that might be the case. Being a supply teacher meant he would have to go where he was needed.

Across the stream, some cows were grazing away like cows do. The birds were making quite the racket in the woods opposite. He closed his eyes and took it all in. This would be the perfect place to heal.

He opened his eyes when he heard Christine sitting down opposite him.

"It's so peaceful," he said.

"Some might say oppressive. Dinner won't be long."

She held her glass up. "Here's to you, Arthur. I hope you'll be happy with us here in Napthwaite."

He raised his glass. "I hope I will be too and thank you for taking a risk with me."

She took a swig of her wine. "Oh, piffle. You had a wonderful reference from your old headmaster."

Poor Mr Gibson. Arthur had left him in the lurch, but he'd understood and had been full of remorse that he couldn't keep his post open.

As if reading his thoughts, Christine smiled. "No regrets now. Whatever has happened is like that water in the stream. It won't flow past here again, no matter what."

At sixty-five, she was an incredibly striking woman with wild grey curls framing her face. She accented these with thick horn-rimmed glasses and a slick of bright red lipstick.

"Everyone seems very lovely here."

Christine made a face. "Oh, it's early days yet. You haven't broken the façade. There are feuds and tensions worthy of a Shakespearean play."

"I hope I manage to stay clear of any of that," he replied. "I think I'll go for an explore up on the hills at the weekend."

"Ah yes, you must go up to Nap Head. The views are stunning. I'd go with you, but my legs aren't quite what they used to be. It's easy enough though. You take the path past Cropper's Farm and carry on up to the top."

"Sounds like a plan."

Christine got up. "I'd better go and sort our food out. Then I'm going to annihilate you at Scrabble. It's all go in Napthwaite."

* * * *

The rest of the week passed with few issues. The more reticent members of his class started to come out of their shells. He had a firm friend in Joel Poole, which seemed to work to his advantage.

At last Saturday morning came and with the sun already high in the sky, he decided to take Christine's advice to discover Nap Head. She had packed him a lunch and sent him on his way.

He had made it a point to respect her space and spent a lot of time in his room. To have the time to read and relax would be good for his recovery. He secretly thought she enjoyed having someone to fuss over again.

But now he had his explorer hat on…although he suspected he might have gone wrong as he walked up an uneven farm track, littered with potholes.

He could have sworn Christine had said to go up here. The track led into a farmyard. This couldn't be right. He dithered for a second in the middle of the yard before the front door of the lovely looking farmhouse opened.

"Come on, girl. You're slow this morning."

A sheepdog sauntered past the owner of the voice who had opened the door and now stopped dead in his tracks when he saw Arthur standing there.

For the second time in Napthwaite, Arthur was floored by the appearance of a ridiculously handsome man. They certainly did breed them well up here. His tan skin and dark curls were everything a BBC drama would dream up.

"Can I help you?" the man said gruffly.

"Yes, I'm off to Nap Head," Arthur replied. "Is it through here?"

The man opened the back door of a Land Rover and his dog leapt in obediently. He walked over to the driver's side.

"No, it bloody isn't. And this is private property."

Arthur frowned. "I'm sure Christine said to go this way."

The man stopped what he had planned to say suddenly. "Christine Carrington?"

"That's right. I'm Arthur Whittaker, the new teacher. I'm lodging with her and she said to come this way."

The handsome farmer seemed to still at the mention of her name.

"Tell you what," he said. "I'm headed up to my top field. I'll give you a lift and point you in the right direction."

"That would be wonderful," Arthur said flashing his best smile.

They got into the Land Rover and the dog forced its way onto the front seat and sat on Arthur's lap, demanding attention.

"Don't mind Madge." The man laughed. "She's a bit of a tart."

Arthur stroked her and tickled behind her ears, which she loved.

"What do they call you?"

"Ed Cropper." He fired up the vehicle and set off out of the yard. "Sorry if I was a bit off with you then. Tourists think it's all right to wander around the place. I even had one walk into my kitchen last year and ask to use the loo."

Arthur made a fuss of Madge. "I'm not a tourist, but I'm not a local yet."

The track led up the hill, past fields with sheep nibbling away. Arthur wondered if the cows outside his bedroom window belonged to Ed.

He snuck a glance at the man driving. He seemed to be one of few words but had a strong profile. Dark stubble covered his face with full lips right in the middle. Little wrinkles were gathering around his eyes, accentuated by those white lines from squinting in the sun. He smelt of the outdoors but not in a bad way.

"I grew up in Blackpool," Arthur said. "I know all about tourists. But you're right. I should have known better and I apologise."

Ed stole a glance at him and they locked eyes. A frisson of excitement ran up his spine. Gorgeous but definitely nervous. Arthur wondered why.

Ed took a deep breath. "I could show you a good walk into Briar Woods if you like. You'll be able to see them up behind the school."

Arthur had noticed the woods and had thought about how he could incorporate them into a lesson.

"That would be wonderful. Are you sure?"

Ed visibly relaxed. "Course I am. I'll come down to Mrs Carrington's Tuesday night if you like. The forecast for next week is pretty good."

"Then I'll sort us some food," Arthur said. "To say thank you."

Ed glanced across at him again. "It's a date then."

* * * *

The week dragged, but, before long, Ed pulled up in the Land Rover and let Madge out. Arthur waved at him from his bedroom window, then heard

Christine opening the front door as he finished his laces.

"Edward. How lovely to see you."

"Good evening, Mrs Carrington."

"I think we're both old enough for you to call me Christine now, don't you?"

Arthur bounded down the stairs and appeared behind her. "Hello, Ed," he said, cheerfully. "I'm ready to explore the hills."

Ed and Christine looked down at the bright pink Converse trainers he had on.

"Haven't you got anything a bit sturdier?" Christine asked.

"Won't these do?"

Ed shook his head. "Looks like we're going to Harrogate then. It's late-night opening. Poole's will be shut. Robert doesn't open past five."

Christine chuckled and stroked Madge, who appeared confused that there were three humans in her company and no one had noticed her. "You boys have fun. I'm out at the parish council tonight. I'll see you later."

They both got into Ed's Land Rover and he set off.

"You don't have to do this, you know," Arthur said. "I can go on Saturday."

"It's only twenty minutes. We won't get a walk tonight, but we can go at the weekend if you like."

"I like," Arthur replied.

They drove along in silence. After a minute or two, Arthur started to fiddle with the radio. "You don't mind, do you?"

"Not at all," Ed replied.

In a second, a pop hit blared out of the speakers. Arthur wound his window down and sang along.

"Did you put aftershave on to go for a walk?" Ed laughed.

"I certainly did," Arthur replied. "I wear aftershave morning, noon and night. Don't you?"

"The sheep and cows don't really care what I smell like."

"No, but you should. I would feel naked if I didn't have a spritz or two." Arthur watched the trees passing. The smell of the countryside filled his nose. Everything seemed to be alive. "It's so beautiful here," he exclaimed, breaking his thoughts. "How lucky were you to have this as a kid?"

Arthur turned, shocked at the sadness on Ed's face. He must have said the wrong thing. "You okay? You looked so sad then."

"Would you like to come for dinner?" Ed blurted out. He blushed crimson red after he'd said it.

"I'd love it," Arthur replied. Arthur hadn't thought Ed would be quite so brave.

"Great. How about Friday?"

"Sounds good to me. I'll bring the wine."

Madge looked up and licked Arthur under the chin, making him giggle. "And a dog treat or two. Goodness me."

"Anything you don't like?"

Arthur thought the situation called for a bit of flirtation. "Oh, I like everything."

Chapter Six

James had only left the pub a minute before and already the sweat had started to trickle down his back. He hated hot nights, knowing he wouldn't get any sleep. The pub had been busy when he'd left. The thick stone walls made it cool and most of the locals knew this. Becky had drafted her new boyfriend, Liam, in to help. Normally James wouldn't leave her, but this day of the month meant parish council, and as chair, he had to attend, complete with inane grin on his face.

He turned up Queen Street towards the village hall, which he knew would be an absolute sweatbox. They had always talked about getting air conditioning, but for the few weeks a year they actually had heat in Yorkshire, it seemed an extravagance. He made a mental note not to sit next to Mrs Turnbull in her standard nylon dress.

To his surprise, Liz came out of the shop, carrying a cardboard tube.

"Oh, hello," she said far too innocently for his liking.

"Are you coming to the meeting?"

She waved the tube at him. "I certainly am."

James could smell trouble, and the number of times it accompanied his sister made him particularly attuned. She had been a wild teenager. Villagers still talked about the time she had been sent home from high school for wearing a punk bondage skirt. The fact she had argued with the teacher that by being black it lay firmly within school uniform rules hadn't helped much.

"I don't want to know."

"I never said a thing. Am I allowed to walk with you?"

He sighed. "Come on then."

Parish council meetings were sacred in the village. Nothing had stopped his father from sitting at the head of the table in the hall. Once his mother had had to celebrate her birthday a day late because they clashed. That had gone down well.

They walked up the street. The village lay pretty quiet, but the unmistakable smell of barbecues permeated the air. His belly growled. He'd only had a cheese sandwich for his dinner.

"Are you still not speaking to Ed?" Liz asked, cutting into his thoughts.

He really did not want this line of questioning before leading a meeting. He wished his sister, just for once, would mind her own business. He curbed his temper — snapping at her would only tell her to dig deeper.

"Of course we're speaking. I've been busy."

She gave him a hard frown, which suggested she knew there was more to this tale and resistance would be futile. Thankfully, the interrogation would have to wait as they walked into the village hall where Mrs Carrington waited.

"Good evening, Chair. Oh, and good evening, Mrs Poole."

Christine, instantly suspicious of Liz's presence, frowned, but Liz just smiled sweetly and sat on the seldom-used public chairs. People tended not to come to the actual discussions of the floral colour scheme for the village or who would be Santa at the village Christmas party. They would find out through word of mouth and generally criticise from afar.

Rob Holdsworth, a big lumbering man who coached the rugby team James played for, followed them in. He sank down in the chair next to James.

"Blimey, it's a scorcher," he boomed. "We might have to cancel training this week. Don't want my fragile lads passing out." He chucked James under the chin.

Mrs Turnbull came in very discombobulated. She sat next to Christine and instantly began wafting herself with the agenda. "Oh my, it's hotter than Mercury today," she exclaimed. She opened her collar and fanned her ample cleavage.

James stared straight ahead as he knew Rob's eyes would be boring into him, threatening to make him laugh.

As usual, Matthew Johnstone made a slightly late entrance. A sprightly older man who lived in Thorpe Hall, the big house down Nap Lane, he owned a lot of land in the area and seemed to think himself lord of the manor. Not a bead of sweat appeared on him as he sat down next to Rob.

"Evening, everyone," he said eventually.

"Evening, Matthew," they all mumbled.

Matthew had done a tenure as chair when James' father had died. But when James had stood against him three years ago and romped it home, Matthew had had to settle for being a regular parish councillor again. This demotion had not gone down too well. He made it a principle to find an alternative view to anything James proposed.

Christine, as secretary, started to rattle through the minutes of the previous meeting. It all went swimmingly. Mrs Turnbull looked pleased as punch when they congratulated her on the appearance of the flowers in the village. She took it all very seriously and would dream up colour schemes starting in January.

"We need to start to think about the fête," Christine said.

"Already? It's not until August," Rob countered.

"Which is only eight weeks away," she replied.

They had the same discussion every year. The fête had a separate committee, but the parish council were obliged to hold a dinner the evening before they officially opened the fête.

"I'll host the curry night again at the pub," James offered.

"Don't you want to do something different?" Matthew said. "Remember that wonderful garden party we had at the Hall when I was chair?"

A ripple of acknowledgement went around the table. James remembered it perfectly well. They had run out of wine in the first hour, the sandwiches had been stale and most of the village had ended up at the pub for a singsong. He'd even roped Ed into helping serve drinks, they were that busy.

The memory of him and Ed working together stabbed at his heart and for a second he thought he wouldn't be able to control the tears. But he fought them down. Would it ever not feel this raw? He couldn't imagine it and wasn't sure he even wanted that.

"I think we'll stick to the curry, Matthew," he managed, noticing the tremor in his voice.

"What a shame. I've got a new gardener you know. He's exhibited at Chelsea."

They all took great interest in the agendas before them. It didn't do to engage with Matthew or meetings could overrun.

"I hope you're getting caterers in," Matthew continued. "I've not heard good things about your place since that excuse for a chef quit last year."

It rankled James that Matthew had a point. Becky tried her best, but she managed to burn things on the outside and undercook them on the inside. He'd caught the quiz team with their own sandwiches last week.

"Mohinder has kindly offered to stand in."

Matthew nodded what must be his approval. "We can't all have London chefs in the family," he said, patronisingly.

"How is William doing?" Rob asked.

A self-satisfied smirk crept across Matthew's face. "Very well thank you. He's talking about opening his own place next year."

"Busy then," Rob continued. "I'm sure he'll manage a visit this year."

The smile fell from Matthew's face to be replaced by an icy stare.

"That leaves us with the section on the agenda for any public contributions," Christine butted in.

Everyone glanced over at Liz who had been waiting patiently, as silent as a church mouse. She cleared her throat and stood then slowly approached the table.

With great fanfare, she unrolled the item from the tube and laid it out in front of the council members. It seemed to be architect plans of some sort.

"What are we looking at here, Mrs Poole?" Mrs Turnbull said. "I've never been good at puzzles."

"These," Liz announced, "are plans to build on my car park. I want to extend the offering I can bring to the village, but I'm restricted by space."

Liz's Aladdin's cave would benefit either from more space or less stock, but this shocked James.

"The car park?" Rob said, aghast. "But people use that to do errands. We don't all live in the village."

"And for the bowling," Matthew piped up.

"Well, technically it is supposed to be for my customers," Liz reminded them.

James knew how much effort it would be taking to keep the annoyance out of her voice.

"It will be quite the blow, no matter what," Mrs Turnbull grumbled. "Our Irene parked there for the whole weekend when she came to stay the other month."

"Anyway," Liz continued, half scowling at her, "this will be a lovely modern glass extension with aluminium struts. The sun will glint off it something lovely."

James frowned. "It's not really in keeping with the village, is it?"

This time Liz couldn't hide her annoyance. "Things move on, James. We're not living on a movie set, are we?"

They all exchanged glances. James hoped that the council would do his work for him and he wouldn't have to go head to head with her.

"Isn't this just a continuation of your ridiculous feud with Kathleen Brockbank?" Christine asked.

Liz started to roll the plans up with gusto. "Of course not. I am an entrepreneur wanting to grow my business. I wouldn't expect you to understand that."

Christine had started to reply when James held his hand up. "There's no need for this. How about emailing us all copies and we can all examine them before the next meeting?"

"Fine," Liz said, going and sitting down but with a glare on her face.

James had a suspicion that he hadn't heard the last of this.

Chapter Seven

Another boiling hot day beat down on the valley. The classroom felt like a furnace and Arthur could barely get any work out of the kids, who were floppy and cranky. In the end, he'd taken them out into the playground, under the shade of the Victorian school building.

They had loved this break in routine and sat in a perfect semi-circle on the wood chippings while he read them a story.

As he got to the end, he saw the usual group of parents arriving to take their charges home. His stomach did a flip when he saw James amongst them.

He slammed the book shut.

"Okay, children. The bell will be going in a few minutes so why don't you go and get your things? I'll be waiting for you out here and anyone who leaves a mess for me to clean up will suffer a fate worse than if the big bad wolf himself appeared."

The children scampered into the school.

"They'll trash the place," James said, approaching him.

"Oh, I think it's good for children to have a little bit of responsibility. They're still learning to trust me so I have to show them the way."

James flashed that dazzling smile that made Arthur's body tingle. He could still see him naked and full of urgency.

"You dared to speak to me then, Mr Brave?" Arthur said.

James had the decency to look embarrassed. "I was out of line the other day. I came over to apologise. You don't have to stay out of my way. In fact, I wondered if you fancied a drink. Not at The King's. Somewhere else?"

Before Arthur could answer, Joel appeared out of nowhere and crashed into James' legs with force.

"Hey there, big guy. You'll knock me over one of these days. I'll have to see if Mr Holdsworth will put you on our rugby team. How was your day?"

"We learnt about Romans."

"You learnt about Romans," Arthur said, shaking his head. "I have no idea who teaches these kids."

James glanced across at another little boy. "Joel, go and tell Philip his mum has popped to your mum's shop. We'll wait with him until she gets here. Go on, scoot."

Joel ran off, leaving them alone. James stared at Arthur expectantly.

"I would love a drink, but I don't think it's a good idea, do you? This job means a lot to me, and I don't want any trouble."

A flash of disappointment spread across James' face, but he quickly masked it.

"Maybe you're right. Either way, you're welcome in The King's. I know you won't say anything."

"There's no danger of that. I don't want people thinking their men aren't safe around me, you know."

James smirked. "I didn't last too long though, did I?"

"Pah," Arthur replied. "You were the one dragging me up that ladder."

"Ah, James. You've met our new teacher then?"

They turned to see Christine approaching them. Her class had joined the throng in the playground.

"I have. He was just telling me how well Joel is doing."

"Are you cooking tonight, or am I? I got confused." Christine was a woman who never shied away from a subject change.

Arthur glanced nervously at James. "I'm actually out for dinner tonight."

She raised an eyebrow. He hadn't done much other than read, teach, play Scrabble and walk in the couple of weeks he'd been here.

"Are you? I guess it's pasta for one then." She frowned across the playground. "Joel Poole and Philip Breton. That had better not be a school football you have there. I've told you before, they stay here."

She shook her head and walked off towards an overly innocent-looking Joel and Philip.

"I'd better follow her," James said awkwardly. "I hope you have a lovely dinner."

Arthur watched him go. The way he filled those jeans, Arthur could watch him walk away all day long.

He forced his thoughts to a more professional space and walked into the school.

His trust had been misplaced when he saw the state of the classroom. Typical that it would happen when he wanted to spend time getting ready to go to Ed's.

By the time he'd got things straight, he had less than an hour. He dashed across the village to Christine's, where he threw on a tight denim shirt and cargo pants that clung in all the right places. Since he'd been in Napthwaite, he'd worn the most sedate clothes in his wardrobe, but he enjoyed putting on something a bit more form-fitting. He glanced at himself in the mirror.

"Still got it, Whittaker," he said before spraying his new favourite cologne all over.

By the time he bounded downstairs, Christine sat in her usual chair with Byron purring away on her lap and a book in her hand.

"Don't you look nice?" she exclaimed. "Ooh and you smell divine. I'm getting a hint of floral and lot of zest."

"Thanks. It's just a meal at Ed's, but any excuse, eh?"

Christine put the book down on the arm of the chair. Byron made a little protest, but when he realised they were staying put, snuggled down.

"He's a lovely man is Edward Cropper, but he's had a hard time. Just bear that in mind."

Arthur smiled. "It's just a meal."

Christine nodded and picked up her book as he dashed out of the house and up the lane. He had to stop himself from running up the old track. He didn't want to turn up all sweaty, but he did feel excited to see Ed again.

Ed must have been watching for him out of the window, because he was standing in the doorway by the time Arthur came round the corner of the barn. For the second time today, Arthur's stomach did a jolt and a juvenile shyness came over him.

Ed had gone simple yet effortlessly handsome in a checked shirt and jeans. Madge poked her head between his legs.

"Fancy seeing you here." Ed smiled.

"Sorry I'm a bit late."

Ed let him pass through into the old kitchen. The smell of cooking hit him as soon as he walked in, and his mouth began to water. He put his bag down on the old kitchen table and produced the bottle of red and packet of dog treats he had picked up at Poole's.

"Presents for everyone."

Ed blushed. "Thank you. You didn't have to do that. I'll get them opened. You go on through to the living room."

Arthur walked through the wooden door into the large lounge. A slate fireplace dominated the room, with a sofa covered in throws, and an old leather armchair. Arthur instantly relaxed. He didn't know what he had expected, but there were some nice touches. It could probably do with a lick of paint here and there, but all in all, he could get right at home here.

Arthur sank onto the comfy sofa and realised he could quite easily fall asleep if left unattended. Madge instantly curled up next to him and started to demolish the chewy treat he'd brought her. It didn't last ten seconds, then she unsubtly put her head on his leg, clearly demanding a stroke.

"Here you go," Ed said nervously, handing him a glass of wine. "Look at her. She thinks anyone who comes in here is her property."

"Quite right too. Cheers," Arthur said, taking a healthy swig. Ed's anxiety had started to rub off on him or perhaps it had been that conversation with James in the school yard. Either way, a decent glass of wine came in perfectly handy.

"We're having lasagne. I know it's a bit boring, but I had a sheep caught in the fence and it took me longer than I thought to free her, so I didn't have much in."

"I love lasagne," Arthur said.

"Good," Ed replied, a nervous smile on his face.

They sat in silence. Arthur examined the ornaments lining the mantelpiece. They didn't strike him as Ed's taste, the figurine of Bo Peep in particular. The house had a lot of stuff in it. He didn't have Ed down as a hoarder. "I didn't expect this place to be so full."

"It's things that belonged to my parents. I haven't got round to having a clear-out."

Arthur glanced to the only photo in the room. It lay in a small frame on the windowsill and showed a couple on a beach somewhere. "What happened to them?"

Ed shifted on the arm of the sofa uncomfortably. "They died. Nearly fifteen years ago now."

"I'm sorry to hear that. You must miss them terribly."

Ed took a sip of his wine. "How was your day?" he asked, making it clear any further comment would be strictly out of bounds.

"Oh, you know, filled with children shouting and bawling. I love it."

Ed shook his head. "Give me sheep or chickens any day. So much easier." His watch beeped and he jumped to attention. "That's it ready. Come on through."

Arthur followed him into the kitchen with his new best friend Madge in tow. She settled at his feet. The kitchen seemed to be an extension of the lounge in that pans hung from the ceiling, old pictures lined the walls and ornaments were on any surface available.

Ed revealed a bubbling-hot lasagne from the oven and placed it down on the table in front of them. Arthur licked his lips.

"That smells amazing. Just as good as in Italy."

Ed reddened around his neck. "Thank you." He noticed Madge trying to be as inconspicuous as possible. "Go on, you. To your bed."

She sloped off to her bed in the corner with doleful eyes and only a toy for sustenance.

"Poor thing has to sit there watching us eat. Doesn't she deserve another treat?" Arthur pleaded.

Ed laughed. "She is the worst sheep dog I've ever known. Don't get me wrong. When she's in the mood, it's great. But if she isn't, nothing will persuade her. Anyone else would have got rid."

Madge ignored the comment and licked her paw.

"I think she's gorgeous," Arthur said.

Ed picked up a large serving spoon from the draining board on the sink before reaching up to the cupboard above the kettle. Madge leapt to attention, more than ready to receive the biscuits that followed.

"She is gorgeous," Ed agreed, rubbing her ear as she crunched away at the unexpected gift.

He plunged the spoon into the pasta and put a generous helping onto Arthur's plate. A bowl of salad and plate with garlic bread filled the table.

"Help yourself."

Arthur piled up his plate. "I've heard about farmhouse meals. Designed to make you waddle home."

"I love to cook. I don't get much chance. Sorry if it's too much."

They dug in. The sharpness of the tomatoes coupled with the creamy bechamel sauce made Arthur groan. "That is amazing," he said, attacking it again with his fork.

"Tell me about you, then," Ed said, beaming. "You're from Blackpool?"

"That's right. Dad runs a fish and chip shop. How stereotypical? Mum is a teaching assistant. They keep nagging me to let them come and see me, but I thought I'd get a bit more settled first." Arthur filled their glasses. "Sorry — look at me helping myself."

"Don't be silly. You brought it."

Arthur tried not to keep shovelling the lasagne into his mouth. If Ed ever gave up farming, he could definitely feed people.

"Napthwaite must be a bit boring after the bright lights of Blackpool," Ed said.

Arthur considered how he would answer this. He didn't want to start whatever this could be on a fib, but he also didn't want to scare Ed.

"Quiet is right up my street at the moment," he said. "I've had a bit of a tricky time of it this year. Men and partying and the like." He noticed Ed perk up at the mention of men. "I need to grow up a bit."

Ed speared a piece of cucumber. "Sounds pretty grown up to me. Just recognising that you need to in the first place is a big step."

Arthur had to admit that he did feel pride at how he'd turned his life around. This time last year he had been going out every night and counting down the days until the school holidays. He and Martin had spent most of them in Ibiza.

"How about you? Born and bred here?"

Ed raised his eyebrows. "I think that's pretty obvious, don't you? I am the epitome of boring."

Arthur didn't like to hear him putting himself down like that. "I don't think you're boring."

Once again that blush covered Ed's face.

Despite his best efforts, he couldn't manage any more food and Arthur reluctantly put his knife and fork down.

"I could eat that every day."

A pleased Ed took his plate.

"You must let me do the washing up," Arthur insisted.

Ed refilled their glasses and sat down again. "You will not. They can soak for a bit. We can sit in there if you like."

"No, it's nice in here. Did you used to have a lot of meals in here with your mum and dad?"

Ed dropped his gaze. "I don't talk about them. Sorry."

Arthur knew he should have taken the first hint and cursed himself for spoiling the atmosphere. He reached across and put his hand on Ed's, who flinched but let it stay there.

"Of course. I'm sorry for being a nosey sod."

Ed looked at him, his eyes moist. "You're not nosey. You're a decent guy."

"So are you."

Arthur planted his lips on Ed's. They kissed. It was so gentle and perfect. Arthur squeezed Ed's hand and let the tingles flow through him. This had been long overdue. Truth be told he'd wanted to do this ever since he had climbed into Ed's Land Rover on that first day.

Suddenly Ed broke away, his hand shooting out from under Arthur's. "I'm sorry."

"Hey, that's okay. I hope I didn't overstep the mark. I just thought—"

"You thought right. I was with someone, for a long time. Now I'm not. It's taking a bit of getting used to."

This surprised Arthur. He had put Ed down as a closet case who would need coaxing out. He hadn't even thought that he might have had history.

Then it struck him.

"James?"

Ed reacted as though someone had fired a gun through the window. "How do you know James?"

"I stayed at The King's Arms the night before my interview. I met him then."

The atmosphere in the room plummeted.

"And how do you know he's…like us?"

Arthur wasn't a liar, and he didn't intend to start now. He knew this might ruin everything, but he had to tell him.

"We had…an experience. Nothing heavy. We got a bit drunk."

Ed stood up from the table. "And you thought you'd come and get me drunk and have an…experience with me as well?"

Arthur reached for him, but he wouldn't be placated. "That's not it at all. Don't be silly. It just happened. I've barely seen him since before today when he picked his nephew up."

"Did you tell him you were coming here?" Ed asked, panic setting in.

"No of course not. Ed, relax."

Madge, obviously sensing tension, rubbed herself against her dad's leg and gave a low growl at this newcomer who seemed to be upsetting him. She might be free with her love, but her loyalty remained true.

"I think it's best if you go."

"Ed."

"Please, Arthur. Please just go."

Chapter Eight

It had been a crazy week at school with a sickness bug sweeping through the village and most of his class being ticking vomit bombs. So far, he hadn't succumbed, but if he didn't pick up the school mop for a while, he wouldn't be unhappy.

In the quiet moments, he had fretted about Ed. He bitterly regretted falling into bed with James so easily, but he certainly didn't regret telling Ed about it. To tell him further down the line would have been worse. Arthur knew how secrets could fester.

He almost turned his ankle on one of the potholes as he walked up the track on Friday evening. He clutched his shopping bag from Harrogate and silently cursed this awful road.

Once in the yard, his stomach churned. This could either be the onset of the bug or nerves. He hoped the latter or things could get seriously embarrassing.

A couple of sheep called to each other across the still summer's evening and the odd bird sang to its friends in the woods above the farm. Other than that, only overwhelming quiet reigned supreme. He didn't think he'd ever get used to the silence in Napthwaite.

In front of the door, he took a second then knocked. Madge made a half-hearted attempt at barking. She really was the worst guard dog he had ever met. He heard movement inside and straightened up.

The door swung open and Ed appeared, handsome as ever with his hair all mussed up like he'd just woken from a nap. Those thick curls seemed to obey only their own rules.

"Oh, it's you."

Arthur hadn't expected to be welcomed with open arms, but he'd hoped for a little more. He held up the carrier bag. "I come in peace."

Warily, Ed took the proffered bag. Inside lay a bottle of aftershave.

"Everyone should have some cologne," Arthur said.

Ed gave the box the once over, then looked at Arthur. "Am I supposed to fall into your arms now?"

"No, but I thought you might at least offer me a cuppa," Arthur replied, hopefully.

Ed's shoulders relaxed, and he gestured into the kitchen with his head. Arthur walked in. Madge sat on her bed and studied him carefully with a low growl. She obviously hadn't forgotten this intruder who had upset her dad.

"You'd probably best chuck her a treat," Ed said, handing him a box while he put the kettle on. "She'll forgive you pretty quickly then."

Arthur threw a generous handful of treats onto Madge's bed and Madge happily vacuumed them up.

Once they had all gone, she settled down and closed her eyes.

Arthur couldn't help but laugh, and to his delight, Ed joined in. Ed put a steaming mug of tea in front of him and sat.

"Go on, then. Tell me how sorry you are you slept with my ex-boyfriend, how it didn't mean anything, blah blah."

Arthur frowned. "Ed, I don't think you're being entirely fair. Firstly, I didn't know he was anyone's ex. Secondly, if I say it didn't mean anything, you'll think I'm a slag, but if I say it meant something, you won't even consider this going any further."

Ed ran his hands through his hair. He seemed tired. "Maybe you're right. I don't know. I'm all over the place at the moment. I'll level with you as James obviously hasn't. He and I were together for years and best friends since I can remember. It all went shit-shaped about a month ago. Then you arrived."

It was typical of him to come to the countryside for rest and recuperation only to find himself in the middle of some relationship warzone. Every fibre in his being told him to finish his tea and walk away, but the vulnerability in Ed's eyes made him want to wrap his arms around him and make it all go away.

"Sounds like you've been through it."

"But so have you and it's not fair of me to treat you like that. I'm sorry. I'm not over James. I know I'm not. If anything happened between *us*, it would be rebound."

Arthur could feel him slipping away again. "Ed, I'm not expecting marriage. I don't even know if I'll be here after this term. I'm on trial, remember. What

I do know is that I'd like to get to know you properly. I like you."

Ed shifted uncomfortably and took a sip of his drink, seemingly burning his lip in the process and wincing. "Well, you're honest. I'll give you that."

"It's my virtue and my downfall most of the time," Arthur replied, blowing on his drink.

"Fine, you have a deal. No promises and no expectations?"

"Deal."

Arthur held his hand over the old oak table and Ed shook it. After these terms had been agreed, what did they do now?

"Aren't you going to smell your present?" Arthur managed eventually.

Ed reached for the aftershave he had put on the table when they'd come in, pulling the cellophane off and taking the bottle out of the black box.

"It's Chanel," Arthur said.

"Makes a change from cow muck and sheep, I'm sure. Why don't you spray it on me?"

Arthur got up and came around the table. He took the bottle from Ed's hand and sprayed it liberally on his neck.

"Smell good, sir?"

"Smells great. What do you think?"

Arthur took in the woody citrusy fragrance. It smelt good, especially on him. Ed snaked his arm around Arthur's waist, pulling him closer towards him. He moved his head and their mouths met like two crashing torrents.

Ed ran his hands down to his ass. Arthur was as hard as a rock now and pawed at Ed's body.

"Come on," Ed murmured.

He took Arthur by the hand and led him through the lounge then practically dragged him up the staircase and into his bedroom, which was a stark contrast to the rest of the house. It felt more like Ed, with a big painting of a foreign scene above the bed and white bed linen. The windows were wide open, letting in the perfume of the grassy fields that lay below.

Ed pulled Arthur's T-shirt over his head, leaning down to kiss his nipples. Arthur ran his hands through Ed's mass of curls. Ed fiddled with his belt buckle, then dropped to his knees and opened his jeans, dragging them and his boxers down to the floor. Arthur's swollen cock stood, inches from Ed's face and glad of the freedom. Arthur kicked off his trainers and socks before stepping out of the rest of his clothes.

"You look amazing," Ed said, taking his body in.

Arthur fell onto the bed, spreading his legs and stroking his cock.

Ed pulled his shirt over his head. His lithe body had the tan of someone who worked outdoors. Arthur could barely wait to explore it.

Ed got rid of the rest of his clothes and crawled on top of Arthur. Their cocks pressed against each other as Arthur wrapped his legs around Ed's waist, his foot grazing his arse.

They kissed, but this time slowly. Ed held Arthur's hands above his head and ground his hips against him. Ed started to kiss his neck, sending a cascade of shockwaves through his body. Arthur had been thinking about this moment all week. He wanted Ed more than he'd wanted anyone for a long time.

He struggled free and they rolled over so he straddled Ed. Leaning back, he took both their cocks in his hand and moved his own hips slowly.

"Oh yes," Ed murmured, closing his eyes.

Arthur reached down and rubbed the pre-cum forming on Ed's cock. He couldn't wait any longer to taste him.

He shuffled down and let his breath fall on Ed's twitching dick. Arthur licked the tip, making Ed moan.

He nuzzled his nose into Ed's balls. The musty smell of him could tip Arthur over. He knew that if he dared touch his own cock, it would be an early finish.

He swiped his tongue up the length of Ed and as he reached the top, he glanced up. Ed stared down at him, willing him to go on. Arthur complied and took his whole cock in his mouth, running his lips down to the base.

Ed speared his fingers through Arthur's blond curls. "Oh God yes."

Arthur had no more resolve and couldn't tease him anymore. He dove his head up and down as he sucked hard, Ed's groans spurring him on. He reached up and tweaked Ed's nipples as he worked his hard cock.

Before he could take him past the point of no return, he let his cock drop and crawled up his body. They kissed furiously, arms wrapping around each other and legs entwining so they were one.

Ed moved him so he lay on top of him, his taut muscular arms making Arthur feel so safe as he and Ed kissed. Ed took hold of Arthur's legs and lifted them onto his shoulders, licking his calf as he did so.

"Fuck me," Arthur pleaded. He couldn't wait any longer to feel this man inside him.

Ed reached over to the bedside drawers and rummaged around, eventually finding lube and a condom.

Arthur watched him as he fumbled with the packet. Even though his whole body cried out for this, the adorable way Ed struggled with the damn thing made his heart dance.

Eventually Ed rolled the condom onto his twitching cock. He ran a lubed finger over Arthur's hole, making him gasp in anticipation. He arched his hips, giving Ed as much access as he needed.

As Ed dove his finger inside him, Arthur closed his eyes. He needed more. He rested his feet on Ed's shoulders.

Ed pushed his cock against him. For a second, Arthur worried he wouldn't be able to take it, but then he got that amazing rush as his resistance disappeared and Ed slid all the way inside.

"Oh God yeah," he cried out, reaching down and pulling at his own cock.

They moved in tandem, Ed pushing himself in and out to be met by Arthur's bucking hips.

"More," Arthur managed.

Ed started to fuck him hard. He lay forward so their lips met, Arthur holding on to his shoulders as he lost himself in the motion. His arse burnt exquisitely as a panting Ed made the bed shake with his pounding.

"I'm going to come," Ed panted.

Arthur forced his lips onto Ed's as his body shuddered like an electrical current had passed through it. Ed gripped Arthur's body as he groaned.

Still breathless, Ed dropped his face against Arthur's neck while the tremors worked their way through his body. His cock still inside, he reached for Arthur's still raging hard-on and started to pull.

Arthur allowed the pleasure to wash over him. With his other hand, Ed tugged at his balls. "Oh, yeah. That's good," Arthur murmured.

He moved his hips in time with Ed's hand. Gripping the headboard, he tensed his whole body. In no time, the pleasure built to a crescendo. The release came at last, and Arthur let out a moan as he came hard in Ed's hand.

Ed disappeared into the bathroom and returned with a towel, throwing it to him to clean himself up. He got into the bed next to Arthur and cuddled into him.

"God, you're sexy," he murmured.

Arthur threw the towel down onto the floor and luxuriated in the feel of someone else's arms around him. It had been such a long time.

Such a long, long time...

* * * *

The alarm clock cut through Arthur's dreams like a knife through butter. Ed brought him close and nestled into the back of his head. "What time is it?" he managed.

"Six."

"Six?"

Ed kissed the back of his neck. "You're in a farmhouse, you know. No lie-ins here."

Arthur took hold of his hand and squeezed it. "Not even for a visiting townie?"

"You can stay here as long as you want, but aren't you supposed to be teaching the little ones?"

Arthur stretched his legs and let his feet rest on Ed's. "It's Saturday, thank you. Even teachers get the odd day off."

Ed extracted himself and started to get out of bed. Arthur spun around and pulled him down.

"Not even half an hour?" he said before kissing him. He could still smell the aftershave and it drove him wild. They had only had about two hours' sleep but Arthur didn't care. He hadn't felt this good in ages.

Ed laughed. "Tell you what. You stay here. I've got to move the cows from Trotters Field to the barn. I'll get that done and come back for breakfast. I need to do it now. It's easier to get them down the road before anyone wants to use it."

Arthur moved off him and lay on the pillows.

"Well, I'm awake now. How about I help you and we can get onto to the fun stuff more quickly?"

Ed raised an eyebrow. "You're going to help me move the cows?"

"How hard can it be?" Arthur said, leaping out of bed. "You got anything I can wear? I'm not getting my designer jeans covered in cow muck."

Ed lent him some clothes and after a quick coffee they made their way out into the chilly morning that daylight had only just begun to grace. The dew lay heavy on the grass and Arthur struggled in Ed's spare wellies that were far too big for him.

Madge dashed ahead of them as they made their way down to the field.

"How many are there?"

"About twenty in this field. We just need to get them up to the barn by the house. Then they can be all toasty and warm."

"Lucky things," Arthur said, remembering that cosy duvet.

"You had the chance to stay in bed," Ed replied, playfully pushing him on the shoulder.

They got to the field running behind the village. The spire of the church pierced the morning mist. Arthur could see Christine's cottage on the far side and thought about his lovely comfortable bed. The things he did on impulse.

The cows started to low quietly when they saw them.

"Right, you get on one side, and I'll get the other. We'll move up and if you get near one, tap her lightly with this." Ed handed him a cane.

"Are they safe?" Arthur asked. He frowned at a cow who ventured very close to him and who didn't seem in the least bit ready to comply.

"For the most part."

Arthur smiled weakly at the cow. "Come on then, Bertha. Let's be having you. You're not going to hurt Arthur, are you?"

The cow he had named Bertha started to move.

"I'm a natural," Arthur declared, beaming.

Madge sat down on the grass and watched the proceedings.

"More than she is." Ed nodded at her.

They managed to get the cows into some semblance of order. Ed handed Arthur a sack of feed.

"You go and stand by that gate and shake this. They'll come to you no problem now they know we're here. Don't let them go the wrong way. I'll cut across the field and meet you at the farm gate."

He patted Arthur on the shoulder and sent him off to the gate with a slap to his arse. True enough, as soon as Arthur started to shake the feed, the cows started to amble towards the gate.

"You look as though you're about to face a bloody firing squad," Ed shouted.

Arthur stuck out his tongue. But the cows were clearly old hands at this and filed obediently out of the field and down the small country lane towards the farm gates. This gave him time to watch Ed run across the field and over the fence just in time for the first cow approaching.

"Your dad is quite the handsome farmer," he told Madge. He remembered Ed's hands on his body last night. The rough hands that worked outside all day long had been so gentle and known exactly what he wanted. He hardened again. "Let's get these cows to bed. I've plans for him."

He and Madge followed the last beast. Ed directed the cows up the farm track and waited for Arthur who bounded up to him.

"I did it," he said, his grin reaching from ear to ear.

"You certainly did." Ed wrapped his arm around his shoulder and kissed him.

Arthur snuggled into Ed. "I could get used to this," he murmured.

"Let's see how you feel about mucking them out later on," Ed said. "Come on—they need to get their breakfast. I fancy something altogether different for mine."

With his arm still across Arthur's shoulders, they walked up the farm track. Out of the corner of his eye,

Arthur saw movement in the woods on the way to the village. He stopped and stared.

"What's up?" Ed asked, following his gaze.

"I thought I saw someone."

He scanned the area again but couldn't see anything.

"Are you getting paranoid?" Ed asked, kissing him again. "It could have just been a deer or something. Come on."

They walked up the track, but Arthur kept staring at the trees. He had definitely seen someone.

Chapter Nine

"You're not allowed to turn around until I say," Ed said.

He had taken Arthur up to Mere Rocks. The best view in all the world. It had been a favourite haunt of his as a kid. Life would be busy on the farm, but he had the run of the valley.

"Better than the top of Blackpool Tower?" Arthur said with a pant.

"Even better," Ed managed. He could have sworn they had made this hill steeper than the days when he used to run up here with Blue, his old dog.

Today Madge was their companion and she kept running ahead then coming back. At last, the path levelled out. Ed took Arthur's hand. "Right close your eyes."

Arthur obeyed. Gently Ed moved him around, so his feet were just on the first rock. It wouldn't do to scare him and make him fall. "Ready?" Ed whispered in his ear.

"Ready," Arthur replied.

Ed removed his hands. The sheer astonishment on Arthur's face made the climb up here worthwhile.

"Oh my," Arthur said.

Below them, Napthwaite nestled in the valley. But the view up towards Holton was the real payoff. Little farms dotted the hillside, with tiny sheep like white clouds set against the green grass.

"Look," Ed said, pointing. "A red kite."

The bird glided through the warm summer air, scanning the ground for prey.

Arthur turned to Ed and kissed him. "Thank you for showing me this. It is wonderful."

They walked to the edge of the rock and sat, their legs dangling. Madge sat too and put her head in Ed's lap. They couldn't hear a thing except for grasshoppers playing their familiar tunes. In the distance a dog barked. Madge's ear twitched.

"I'm glad you gave me another chance," Arthur said.

Ed reached for his hand. "Me too."

They sat in silence for a little longer.

"Can I ask you something?" Arthur said, eventually.

"Of course you can."

"Why did you and James break up?"

A flash of unease ran through him. He hated that James and Arthur had slept together. He also hated he didn't know who he was more jealous of. How could he get this across without sounding so bloody serious? "We wanted different things in the end," he managed.

"What did you want?"

Ed leant on the ancient rock. "I want a future with someone. I want to be proud of who I am and who I'm with."

Arthur frowned. "What's wrong with that? Everyone wants that."

"Not James Durkin." Ed laughed bitterly. "He wants to be the perfect pub landlord."

"Yes, he was terrified I would tell someone. You know, about what happened."

"Sounds like James."

The silence fell again. A butterfly stopped for a rest on the rock in front of them before fluttering off.

"It bothers you, doesn't it? Me and James."

Ed ran his hand through his hair. "Of course, it does. James is a force to be reckoned with. Everyone knows when he's in a room. I'm just poor Ed who follows him around. For once, I wanted something to be for me."

Arthur shifted forward and scratched Madge behind the ear before letting his hand rest on Ed's thigh. "This is just for you. I don't think nonstop about anyone else but you."

Ed kissed him. He couldn't get enough of kissing those gorgeous full lips. "What about you?"

Arthur rested his head on Ed's shoulders. Ed could smell the spicy tones of his aftershave as he nuzzled him. He seemed to have a different one every day.

"Oh, I've had a shit year," Arthur said. "I'll summarise it for you. Bad break-up, shit friends, hard partying, major wobble, out of circulation for a few months."

It sounded pretty intense. Ed presumed by 'hard partying' Arthur meant drugs but didn't like to push him. He would tell him in his own time. "Out of circulation?"

Arthur seemed to be picking his words carefully. "I went to stay somewhere for a bit to get myself together. It's been hard."

"Sounds like we've both had a bit of a rough time," Ed said eventually.

"It does, doesn't it?"

"I propose we spend a bit of time caring for each other and putting it behind us."

Arthur took hold of his hand. "I second that."

Madge licked his neck eagerly.

"I think that motion is carried."

By the time they got to the farm, even Ed's feet were aching. They had walked for hours up on the hills. He wanted to show Arthur everything. Seeing the place through his eyes was magical. He and James knew it like the back of their hands—he'd never experienced this before.

"I'm so glad I came here," Arthur said.

"Me too." Ed winked.

They were lying top to tail on the sofa. Ed massaged Arthur's feet. As soon as they'd got in, they'd showered and had spent the last two hours lazing around in their boxers.

"That feels so good," Arthur said, a lazy smile on his face. "You've nearly killed me today."

"It's been a nice day though, hasn't it?"

"One of the best ever," Arthur decided. "But it's not over yet."

He ran his foot across Ed's crotch, making his cock spring instantly to life. The touch of this guy seemed to cast a spell on him. "I thought you were exhausted," he said, raising an eyebrow.

Arthur sat up, pulling his feet out of Ed's reach. He ran his hands down his body and under the waistband of his boxer shorts. Ed licked his lips, watching him. Arthur began massaging his cock — Ed could see it hardening underneath the white cotton and his own cock begged to be released from his black boxers.

As if reading his mind, Arthur got up onto his knees and did the honours. Ed's cock jutted out, glad of the freedom. Arthur ran his finger along the tip and the slight touch gave Ed shivers.

Arthur moved so their lips were almost touching but not quite, Ed's heart rate speeding up as Arthur's soft breath mingled with his own.

Eventually their lips grazed each other, their tongues slowly connecting. His body quivered at the contact. Ed grabbed Arthur by the shoulders and Arthur straddled him, landing kisses on his mouth, face and neck.

The muscles in Arthur's back contracted as he held on to Ed. He ran his hands down to the waistband of his underwear and beyond, cupping both his cheeks.

When they came up for air, Ed teased at the top of his boxers. Arthur stood and let them fall to the floor.

His slim waist and pale, hairless body invited Ed's kisses. He sat on the edge of the sofa and buried his face in Arthur's stomach. Arthur stroked his curls.

Ed soon stood and Arthur made sure his boxers joined his on the floor. Their cocks pressed together as their bodies entwined again. Arthur kissed as though he'd never kiss him again and Ed loved the intensity.

Ed sank on the sofa and Arthur knelt, taking Ed's cock in his mouth. The heat made Ed gasp. He gripped the sofa arm as Arthur moved up and down his cock, maddeningly slowly. It was exquisite torture.

Just as he thought he could take no more, Arthur sped up. Ed matched him, moving his hips at the same speed.

"Oh yeah," he moaned. He ran his hands through Arthur's blond curls. Arthur tugged at his balls and sucked hard.

Then Ed's orgasm exploded in Arthur's mouth, the cum draining from him making him shudder. Arthur sat on his haunches, licking his lips.

"You taste amazing," he said, need still in his eyes. "Come here."

Arthur stood and Ed spun him around by the hips and drew him close so Arthur sat on his lap. Reaching down, he took hold of Arthur's throbbing dick and started to pull.

He wanted to make him come so badly. Arthur steadied himself, holding on to Ed's leg. Ed kissed his neck, twisting his nipple with his free hand and making him moan all the more.

It took no time before Arthur's body tensed and he let out a cry, his cum filling Ed's hand.

They lay there for a second, Ed enjoying the feeling of being so close to another human. He had missed the feel of a body next to his.

"You're amazing, Ed Cropper," Arthur said, kissing him before getting up in search of a towel.

Ed watched him digging around the washing piled up on the dining chair. He loved that Arthur felt at home enough to do that already.

Arthur threw him the towel. "What?"

"Nothing. I'm just happy. That's all." Ed smiled. Arthur sank down on the sofa next to Ed who planted a kiss firmly on his cheek. "You make me happy."

Arthur grinned. "This is our time and no one is going to fuck it up for us."

Chapter Ten

"Hello, hello," James shouted from the back door.

"I'm almost ready," Liz replied.

A first time for everything. Dean and Joel sat at the table playing a game amongst dirty plates, some schoolbooks and a pile of all-weather gloves which James presumed were headed for Robert's outdoor pursuits shop.

"Where's Bobby Boy?"

Liz liberally applied some mascara. "In the shop finishing up. We've started opening until seven Thursdays, Fridays and Saturdays."

James glanced at Dean who shook his head. No prizes for guessing what had prompted this decision.

"Your move, Kathleen," James laughed, giving Joel a hug.

"Pah," Liz replied, grabbing her trusty cardboard tube. "Any retaliation will be a bit stupid once this bad boy gets passed."

James sat at the table, moving Joel's school bag off the chair. "I wouldn't be too cocky. Word in the pub is a few people are up in arms about it."

Liz sank down in the other chair and stole a crisp from Dean.

"Have you not had your dinner yet?" Dean asked, trying to cover the packet with both hands.

"Are you serious?" Liz said to James, ignoring her son. "Typical of this village to stand in the way of progress. I don't know why people are so scared of change. At least you'll support me."

Her face suggested that trouble would be tenfold if James dared take any other path. He just smiled sweetly at her.

"That means I only need two more on my side. I wonder who to pick."

"Mum, that's hardly a fair fight," Dean exclaimed.

Liz distracted him by giving him a sloppy kiss on the cheek and grabbing another crisp. "All's fair in business and crisps."

James looked at Joel.

"I haven't got any. Do you know how much salt is in those? We learnt about it at school," said his nephew, obviously guessing his thoughts.

James winked at Liz. The two boys couldn't be more different. Dean, a thoughtful lad who hadn't really blossomed yet, didn't seem to have any ambition. Joel, on the other hand, would go far, a ball of energy who devoured books and excelled at school. The small village wouldn't contain him for long.

"Hey, guess who's back in the land of the living?" Liz said, glancing at the clock.

"Who's that?" James asked. It wasn't often Liz had news that hadn't reached him behind the bar, but he let her play the game.

"Ed."

James' whole body contracted at the name. "Really?" he said as nonchalantly as he could muster.

"Yes, buying a box of chocolates if you please. I guess we know why he's been on the missing list all these weeks. He must have got himself a lass. Poor James did get jealous after all."

Thankfully the clock struck seven. "We'd best be going," James said, getting up.

"A lass? Yeah right," Dean muttered, rolling the dice.

Liz's head spun round at an alarming rate. "What do you know of it?"

Dean moved his counter around the board, overtaking Joel's, much to his annoyance. "Because the other morning I took Belle out and saw him and a certain local teacher looking ever so close."

"Mrs Carrington?" Joel piped up.

"You—shop, now," Liz ordered.

"What?"

"Tell your dad I said you could have a lolly. Scram."

Joel didn't need telling twice and scrambled out of the room.

"Right, spill," Liz demanded, turning to Dean.

"Nothing more to it. Him and Mr Whittaker were smooching all over each other. They'd brought the cows down from Trotters Field, but I don't think their minds were on it. If you know what I mean."

Liz glared at James, who worried that his heart would burst out of his chest and land right there on the kitchen table. "Do you know about this?" she asked him.

"How would I know about it? I haven't seen him for weeks."

Liz glared. "Ed Cropper is no more gay than you are. We should know. He's been practically part of the family for years. I knew there was something about that Arthur Whittaker I didn't like. Coming here and confusing people."

"Mum, I don't think it works like that," Dean said. The amusement had left his face. He glanced nervously at James.

"How would you know? You're only twenty-two. There are a lot of different people out there, Dean. They can prey on someone's weakness. Right, come on you. We've a parish council meeting to get to."

On weak legs, James followed his sister out of the house. His mind cast back to Arthur naked in his bed. Now he would be doing that in Ed's bed, a bed that they had shared for years. He desperately wanted to swerve the meeting, but it would be pretty obvious if he cried off now.

Liz carried on banging on about Arthur and Ed as they crossed the road to the village hall. The rest of the council were already seated at the table when they came in.

"At last. I nearly sent a search party out for you," Rob said with a frown when he saw Liz enter behind James.

James sat down at the head of the table, grateful for the chair. It seemed a struggle to get his body to do what he wanted it to.

"We'd best get started," Christine said. "Mrs Cleghorn needs to set up for Zumba in half an hour.

We really must get things sorted for the fête. Mr Durkin, will you be judging again?"

All eyes fell on him.

"Yes, whatever you need." He couldn't pull himself together. A hundred different emotions fought for supremacy inside him and none of them were good. "Let's just get on with the agenda, shall we?"

Christine started to read out the minutes from the last meeting. James couldn't take in her words. Ed and Arthur? He glanced across to Liz in the public chairs. She also seemed lost in thought, but a wry smile had started to creep across her face.

"The first item is Mrs Poole's potential extension," James said, casting an eye on the agenda.

Liz got up, brandishing her cardboard tube.

"There's no need to lay it out again, Mrs Poole. I think we all saw enough last time." Christine sighed. "And I for one am against. This will ruin our lovely village."

"I agree," Matthew piped up. "The last thing we need is that monstrosity scaring off visitors."

Liz's proud face crumpled in disappointment.

"I'm sorry, Mrs Poole, but I have to agree also," Mrs Turnbull said, sympathetically. "Where do you propose your customers will park? I absolutely will not have my rear ginnel blocked."

Rob turned his guffaw into a cough.

"This is progress, ladies and gentlemen," Liz continued. "We can easily build a car park in one of the fields. I'm sure Barnes Field would suit and it's on the outskirts of the village."

"And right opposite the beck from my house," Christine said with indignation "No, thank you."

Liz started to circle the table like some bird of prey. James couldn't bear to watch.

"Your house? I dread to think about your house," Liz muttered.

Christine frowned. Another one who had never stood down from a fight, she stared hard at Liz.

"It's not like you to be subtle, Mrs Poole. If you've something to say, why don't you spit it out?"

Liz stopped at the foot of the table, right opposite from James. "Very well. That person who lodges with you. Not only is he responsible for the welfare of our children, but he is having unnatural sex with a member of this village. A male member of this village, I might add. Instead of looking down on me, a normal family woman just trying to further her business, why don't you do something about that…that pervert under your roof?"

Christine slammed her hand down on the desk. "What Mr Whittaker does in his own time is no business of mine and certainly none of yours."

"Hear, hear," Rob added.

"Oh, easy for you to say, Rob Holdsworth," Liz said loudly, clearly on a roll. "Your kids are practically grown. My son is very impressionable. I don't want a whole generation of this village growing up to be…"

"Free?" Christine interjected.

"Now just one second." Matthew glanced from one woman to the other. "I think we should hear Mrs Poole out. As a parent, she has a valid concern who is teaching her child."

"My grandson is in his class too," Mrs Turnbull said.

Christine turned to James for support, but he looked down. He had no idea what to do. "This isn't a parish council matter," he mumbled weakly.

"It is a village matter," Matthew said.

"What are you going to do? Run him out of town with torches and pitchforks?" Rob asked, his face bright red with anger. "I would have thought you of all people might have learnt a bit of tolerance in your old age."

Matthew scowled across the table. They had long been foes and this would take no encouragement to ignite like a petrol bomb.

"I'm sure I haven't the faintest idea what you're talking about. I will get onto the director of education, that's what I'll do."

Rob stood. "You nasty piece of work. You're going to ruin a young man's career because of your filthy bigotry? Tell me, when did you last actually see William?"

"Don't you bring my son into this," Matthew said, standing also.

Christine stood too and raised her hands. "No one will be ruining anyone's career. What you are proposing is illegal. I would suggest you read up on The Equality Act 2010."

Mrs Cleghorn came into the room and stopped dead at the scene being played out in front of her. "I'm ever so sorry, I thought you'd be done by now. My ladies are waiting outside."

The standoff broken, Matthew started to gather his things. "I suggest we discuss this, at length, at the next meeting."

"I will be more than happy to explain to you then as now, your prejudices have no place in modern society," Christine replied.

"And as for my planning?" piped up a now innocent-looking Liz.

"Do what you like," Christine said, sweeping out of the room.

The rest all stared at James. "I guess it wouldn't hurt to put some notices up. See if anyone has any objections before the end-of-July meeting."

Liz beamed at the rest of them. James couldn't wait to get out of there.

"Are you coming in for a brew?" she asked as they walked home.

James spun around. "Does it not even bother you? What you just did in there?"

She held her hands up in mock protest. "Don't tell me you're going to join the woke brigade. He deserves it."

"And Ed? Does he deserve it?"

"You lie with dogs, you get fleas," she replied with a sniff.

He couldn't be bothered to argue. Leaving Liz in the street, he bolted down to the green and into the car park. He fired up his car and drove out of the village towards Ed's farm.

He noticed Ed and Arthur sitting out in the garden, taking in the summer evening, as he drove up the track. By the time he got out of the car, Ed had stood, frowning. James let himself in the gate and walked up the path.

"Oh, it's you," Ed said. It caught in James' chest that he would greet him with such disdain.

"Yep, certainly is. Do you have a second?" James asked. He wanted things to be civil but the conversation was not going to go that way. No matter how hard he tried.

Ed shifted uncomfortably. "Well, I…"

Jealousy gripped James like a vice when he saw Arthur sitting on the bench in sweatpants and hoodie, looking so at home it made him want to vomit. James remembered those sweatpants when they were on the floor of his lounge and Arthur naked in his bed.

"James," Arthur said.

He tried to put his bravest grin on but knew he'd failed miserably. "The very same. I came here because I had to tell you."

Ed looked well. His Gran Canarian tan had faded but James detected a glint in his eye. It hurt James to admit it, but Ed seemed happy.

"Tell us what?" Ed asked.

"Your secret's out."

Ed put his hand on Arthur's shoulder.

"We haven't got a secret," Arthur replied, putting his hand on Ed's.

"Either way, the village knows you're together and some of them aren't happy about it."

Arthur laughed. "Are you joking?"

This guy had no idea how villages worked, but Ed did. His ashen pallor told James all he needed to know about his mindset. "Who? Who isn't happy about it?"

James sighed. He had dreaded this question. He knew he had to level with them. Things might be shit between him and Ed, but they had shared so much. He couldn't let him walk into the situation blindly. "Liz is the leader, it seems."

"What the fuck? Are you joking?"

James shook his head. Being at the farmhouse overwhelmed him. He could hear the words coming out of his mouth and it all seemed like a bad TV drama. Why couldn't things have stayed as they were? "She laid into Christine at the parish council meeting tonight. Seems Matthew is going to ring the director of education."

Arthur sunk down onto the bench. Madge leapt up next to him and put her head in his lap. He absentmindedly stroked her, causing sharp waves of pain to wash over James. "I can't believe this. Have we gone back in time or something?"

James couldn't help but feel sorry for him. "They won't get anywhere. The law is on your side. Fuck them."

"You're going to stop her though, aren't you, James?" Ed asked.

James started to retreat to the gate. He had to get out of here. Why had all eyes suddenly fallen on him? He turned around and the look of absolute loathing on Ed's face cut deeply into him. James glanced at Ed gripping his new lover's shoulder for support. He had never felt more unwelcome in his life. He needed to get out of there.

"Aren't you, James?" Ed repeated.

Pulling the gate open as though his life depended on it, he just managed, "I'll leave you to it," before dashing out to the yard, letting the gate slam shut behind him.

"You're a fucking coward," Ed screamed after him.

James jumped into his car, shutting the door to keep out the barbed words from the love of his life.

He hurtled out of the yard, making a vow that he would never come back.

Chapter Eleven

Pounding dance music blared out of the speakers. Ed could almost feel it in his chest. He had often wondered about the Leeds gay scene but had never plucked up the courage to actually try it. As it turned out, it wasn't so different to Gran Canaria.

Arthur stood talking to a couple of guys in the scrum at the bar. He marvelled at how confident Arthur had been when they'd come in — finding a place to sit almost instantly then wandering up to the bar as though he owned the place. Now he'd made some friends.

Ed tried to relax. The pub was heaving, and people crowded onto the street. It looked like a regular pub from outside, only the neon-lit *Showbar* sign gave it away.

A drag queen, spilling out of her sequined bodysuit, lip-synced to a disco classic on the small stage at the back. She wasn't bad, and the crowd were lapping it up.

Ed frowned as the smell of a hundred different colognes filled the air, masking the stale alcohol and cigarette smoke that drifted in through the door.

Arthur came to the table holding two pints and squeezed onto the faded velvet seat next to Ed. He looked incredible in a tight black T-shirt and shorts. Ed had agonised for days over what to wear and had opted for his usual jeans and checked shirt. He felt woefully underdressed, but Arthur hadn't seemed to notice.

"Cheers," Arthur said.

Ed held his pint up. "Here's to my first visit to a UK gay bar."

Arthur shook his head. "I can't believe that. You're thirty-two, for goodness' sake."

"Who are your mates?" Ed asked, hoping he didn't sound jealous.

"They're not mates. Just got chatting in the queue," Arthur said, glancing over at the bar.

A group of young men swanned in like they owned the place. At easily ten years younger, they seemed more worldly wise than Ed had ever been.

"Yes, well, James refused to do the scene. Don't get me wrong. We've been to Sitges and Gran Canaria, but he always panicked someone would see him in this country."

Arthur stared around the place. "I don't think they get many from Napthwaite in here."

The number of times they had had that argument. Thinking about James brought up so many emotions. He shouldn't have sent him away like that.

"Don't tell me you're feeling guilty again," Arthur said with a frown.

Ed sighed and took another swig of his pint. "It must have taken a lot for him to come and warn us like that."

Arthur let out a huff. "It would be better if he'd muzzle that sister of his. Christine collared me before I came to meet you tonight. Apparently Liz has started a whispering campaign in the playground. A couple of the other parents mentioned something to her. They're worried. She's going to do damage before this is out."

Ed took hold of Arthur's hand. "I don't know what's got into her. We were like the Three Musketeers when we were little. She's a gobshite, but I never thought she'd do this. What did Christine say?"

Arthur laughed bitterly. "She told them to bugger off."

They sat in silence. The drag queen had started a comedy routine and had everyone eating out of the palm of her hand. Ed appreciated the chance not to speak about things for a while.

"Do you miss him?"

"Sorry, what?"

"James. Do you miss him?"

Ed pondered this for a second. "Of course I do. We've been best friends since we were four."

Arthur stared hard at him as if trying to solve a puzzle. "You know what I mean."

Ed really didn't want James interrupting their first proper date. He kissed Arthur. It felt so wonderful to be able to kiss in a public place.

"Honestly? Yes, but that's nothing to do with you. You have made me feel so free."

Ed put his hand on Arthur's leg. "Let's forget about it. For tonight. I will fix this, I promise."

Arthur clasped his hand over Ed's, but the look on his face seemed almost defeated. Ed hated seeing him like this. It had been all quiet in the village for a week. But whispers couldn't always be heard — it didn't mean they weren't there.

"James was so lucky and threw it away. I wish I had that history you two share."

James had left a gaping hole greater than their history. Ed missed James' strong arms, the way he just made things happen, and when he had seen him standing at the door looking so sad, he had desperately wanted to hold him tight.

Even thinking like that while he was sitting with Arthur sent waves of guilt washing over him. He adored having that slim body next to him in bed. Arthur brought such optimism and experience into his life. He pushed him to do things like this that he would never have dared on his own.

He wished he could just split himself in two and be done with it. "We can make our own history."

"That's true but you've never really asked me much about my life before here," Arthur said.

"I like us being in our bubble. Anyway, I know that your mum works in a school and your sister is in London."

Had he really avoided showing much of an interest in Arthur's life? He didn't know how to do this. He had only had James and they had known everything about each other before they'd even locked lips.

"I don't know anything about your parents though. Why do you clam up whenever I try to speak to you about them?"

Ed did not want to have this conversation punctuated with disco beats and flashing lights. "I never speak about them. With anyone. End of story."

"Ed…"

"I said end of story."

A ruckus started at the bar. The drag queen stopped mid-flow. Arthur and Ed's drinks went crashing to the floor as the table got upended by security dashing in through the door. The bouncers grabbed the two guys Arthur had been talking to at the bar and physically dragged them out of the pub.

"You're not fucking dealing in here," one shouted as the two guys tried to fight to free themselves.

The pub instantly resumed its atmosphere as the door banged. Arthur grabbed his coat.

"Come on. I'm not in the mood for drag queens. Let's find somewhere to dance."

Ed followed him onto the street, trying to ignore his soggy socks thanks to two practically full pints falling on him.

"Did you know they were dealers?" he demanded.

Arthur made a face. "You seem to think they're long-lost friends of mine. Not everyone knows everyone else in the big world, Ed. I told you, I was just passing the time at the bloody bar. Jesus. You don't like me asking questions, but you don't mind interrogating me."

They were on their first proper date, and they just seemed to be upsetting each other with every word.

"Can't you see how this is for me?" Arthur continued. "When I came to bloody Napthwaite, I just wanted some peace. Instead, I'm caught in between you two and am public enemy number one to the rest of the village."

Ed took him in his arms and to his horror, Arthur started to sob.

"Hey now. Come on."

Arthur held on to him tightly. "I'm starting to develop feelings for you, Ed. But how can we go anywhere if the ghost of bloody James is haunting us?"

Ed could see their night out ending up in tatters. "My parents died, and it was the hardest thing I've ever had to deal with. I know that it's good to talk, but that's not how I do it. I can't help that I knew James then, but I also won't open it all up just to help you with your jealousy."

Arthur dried his eyes. "I'm being unreasonable. You shouldn't have to. I guess it's his rotten sister making me stressed."

"I don't really fancy the pub now, do you?" Arthur said sadly.

"I could treat you to a bag of chips for the train home?" Ed suggested.

Arthur nodded and they changed direction, heading towards the station.

"Developing feelings for me, eh?" Ed said at last.

"Maybe," Arthur answered, shyly.

"Feeling's mutual."

Arthur grabbed him and kissed him hard. Ed returned the kiss, his hands running through Arthur's soft locks.

Arthur looked him in the eye. "You're right. Let's make our own world. Fuck James and his manky sister."

They walked to the station in silence. Ed admired Arthur's defiance, but he knew that Liz had the bit between her teeth. It would take more than some carefully placed words to fight her off. He wanted to protect Arthur from this but had no idea how. There was only one person who could stop her, but his silence spoke volumes.

What on earth are we going to do?

Chapter Twelve

The little bag full of white powder had been burning a hole in his pocket all weekend. He hated himself for having given in and bought it. Three times he'd held it above the toilet, desperately wanting to just flush it away, but each time had failed.

Now he found himself here again. Christine had a late governors' meeting. No one would know if he just had one little line. He had almost run home after school, feeling people watching him.

"No," he said out loud.

He might not have the strength to throw the coke away, but he did have it to face Liz Poole. Stashing the bag in his underwear drawer, he caught his reflection in the mirror. "You can do this."

His heart racing as though he had snorted a line, he walked into town. *Just because she's lived here all her life doesn't give her anymore right to be here than me.* Reaching the shop, he filled his lungs, let the air flood out and pushed open the door.

The bell rang.

Liz stood at her captain's position at the till by the door. She looked slightly taken aback when he came in. He let her eyes follow him as he picked up a basket and put a couple of items in. Satisfied, he walked over to her and put the basket down.

"Do you want a bag?" she said, a face like thunder.

"Yes, please."

She unfolded the bag as though it contained a live animal and with a sigh, picked up the first item.

"Nice day for it," Arthur said with a smile.

"Depends what 'it' is," she replied, throwing his eggs into the bag.

"I suppose you're right. I only have dinner in the conservatory planned so I think we're good."

Liz scanned his peanut butter and threw it into the bag.

"I hear you're worried about me," Arthur said as calmly as he could.

The directness seemed to shake her, and she focused on putting the shower gel through the scanner.

"You have no need to," Arthur continued. "The only thing you need to know about me is that I will bring out the best in your son. I give you my solemn promise."

Liz slammed the shower gel into the bag and hit the key on the till. "Nine pounds forty please."

"Mrs Poole—"

"Nine pounds forty, please."

Rage swirled around inside him like a torrent. He wanted to scream *hypocrite* in her face. He wanted to show her the hurt inflicted. He wanted to break down the stony façade she had and get to the bottom of this hatred.

Instead, he took his wallet out and handed her a ten-pound note.

She slammed it into the register then stopped. "You don't fool me. Your type will try to teach our kids all the things that they think are right and we will have no say in it."

It hit him like a whip. He had experienced homophobia before but never so raw. "What a disgusting thing to say," he managed. "What a spiteful nasty bitch you must be."

She reared up as though she had been stung. "Oh, I've never heard such language in all my life. I knew you weren't as nice as you made yourself out to be."

"How can I be nice when a shrivelled shrew like you is trying to ruin my career?"

Almost on the verge of tears, she glanced past him. "See, ladies, this is what they're like when they're exposed."

He spun round to see Ruth Thompson and Caroline Burton looking agog at him. They were mothers of children in his class and so far, he'd got on very well with them. How could he have been so stupid? With tears in his eyes, he grabbed the bag and ran out of the shop.

"I'll put the change in the charity box, shall I?" Liz called after him.

Once he got out on the street, the tears pricked at his eyes. He didn't know where to go. If he went to Christine's, he'd be tempted, and he refused to let her ruin any more of his day.

Instead, he found himself walking to the farmyard and banging on the door.

No answer.

It stood to reason. The June sun shone down. Ed would be out working somewhere. He got out his phone and dialled.

"Hey, handsome," Ed answered.

"Hey." He couldn't keep the tremor out of his voice.

"What's the matter?"

Arthur burst into tears. "Everything."

"Where are you?"

"Your place."

"I'll be there in ten minutes."

Arthur finished the call and sank down on the floor, his back against the door, and let the tears flow.

By the time Ed arrived, he'd pretty much exhausted them, but seeing him leap out of the Land Rover, so worried, and Madge following at his heels, set him off again. Ed crouched and took him in his arms.

"Come on, love," Ed said soothingly.

Madge licked the tears off Arthur's face and he couldn't help but giggle.

"I'm sorry. It's all getting too much. They were all gossiping about me at home time. Christine thinks it's best if I don't do playground duty and now I've made things ten times worse."

He told Ed about his run-in with Liz. They hadn't moved from sitting against the door. Ed had his arms wrapped around him.

"She's a bitch and she deserved it," Ed said venomously.

"Not in front of parents though."

"Oh, don't worry about Ruth and Caroline. They don't have much love for Liz."

It made him feel marginally better, but it still didn't make him feel good. Ed picked up the carrier bag, peering in.

"Eggs and shower gel. Well, that's not going to make much of a dinner, is it?"

Arthur wiped his eyes. "I wasn't really focusing on shopping."

Ed got up and held his hand for Arthur, pulling him up gently and kissing him.

"Let me get showered then we'll nip to the shop and get something to go with these eggs."

Arthur gripped him tightly. "I'm not going to her place."

Ed hugged him again. "Relax. We'll go to Brockbank's. She's doing cheese and some veg. I'll make us an amazing omelette, plus we'll piss Liz off to boot."

Arthur allowed Ed to lead him into the lounge and sit him gently down on the sofa. Madge leapt up and cuddled into him.

Ed turned to her. "I'm leaving you in charge, lady. Mission is to cheer him up. Got it?"

He went up the stairs. Ed really was an amazing man. Arthur had invaded his life and Ed had welcomed him with open arms. Arthur reached down and stroked Madge's tummy. He must have dozed off. He opened his eyes to a kiss from Ed.

"I let you sleep for a bit, but my stomach can't last much longer."

His handsome rugged face took Arthur's breath away and he went in for a deeper kiss. "Thank you for being wonderful."

"All in a day's work," Ed said. "But I've worked up an appetite. Do you want to stay here and I'll go into the village?"

Arthur stood. "I think I'll come with you. I wondered if I could stay here tonight?"

Ed wrapped his arms around him. "You'd better. I'm not letting you go until the morning."

Arthur needed to feel the security. "I'll have to pick up my work clothes."

They walked into the village. Nervously, Arthur glanced around when they turned the corner onto Queen Street. It had got to nearly seven and all the shops were closed, save for Brockbank's.

As soon as they walked in, Kathleen Brockbank stared straight at him. A big woman, she also rarely left the shop. She preferred to get her gossip from her customers. In fact, Arthur had only met her a couple of times, but she evidently knew him.

"Hello there, Ed," she said. "Mr Whittaker."

"Good evening, Kathleen," Ed said, defiantly.

Ed picked up some cheese and wilting spring onions from the tiny grocery section Mrs Brockbank had set up to irk her rival. "It won't be very exciting, but it will fill a gap." He put them down on the counter and picked up the local newspaper, adding it to his pile.

"Very wise to come down when the dust has settled," Mrs Brockbank said, pointedly looking at Arthur who knew he would be blushing.

Ed frowned. "Surely you're not defending Liz Poole?"

Kathleen laughed. "Not me, love. You two do whatever makes you happy. You're welcome in here."

Ed relaxed. "Sorry, Kathleen. It's been a rough few days. Can you add it to my paper bill? I've come without my bloody wallet. What do you mean, the dust settled?"

Kathleen reached for the ancient clipboard with pencil attached by grubby string. She started to mark up the items. "I meant once they're all at the meeting."

The atmosphere changed in an instant. Arthur desperately wanted to get out of there, having no appetite for trouble, but Ed's face suggested he had other ideas.

"Meeting?"

"Yes, on the village Facebook group. Liz fair whipped up a frenzy on there this afternoon after your little...run-in. They're all meeting at the pub now. You know, to discuss things."

Ed didn't wait to hear any more. He grabbed Arthur's hand and half dragged him out of the shop. As they turned onto the green, Arthur saw a crowd of people through the window of the pub.

Arthur made him stop. "This is a really bad idea."

"You're probably right but I'm not having it. You can either come with me or not."

Ed marched towards the pub. Arthur ran after him. He refused to let Liz feel victorious that he had others fight his battles for him. Ed opened the door and Arthur walked through.

James stood behind the bar and went as white as a sheet when he saw them come in.

"Arthur...Ed..."

A group of about fifteen villagers, some he recognised from the playground and others he'd only seen around, were sitting in a semi-circle around the dormant fireplace.

Liz stood facing them and held up an A4 print of Arthur from the Leather Fest in Blackpool last summer. To his shame he had on a leather harness and leather shorts. He remembered Martin daring him to wear them. He froze.

A vicious smile spread across Liz's face when she saw him. "Ah, here he is now. Our wholesome primary school teacher. Perhaps you can explain this?"

Ed stormed over to her and ripped the picture from her hands. "Where did you get this?"

Arthur glanced at James who stood transfixed, staring at his sister and his ex-lover.

Liz sat down. "It's amazing what you can find on Facebook these days."

The other people at the meeting had the decency to look embarrassed.

"Aren't you lucky we didn't have it in the days when you used to carry on with anyone with a pulse?" Ed said through clenched teeth.

She looked as though nothing in the world could bother her. "I wasn't in charge of impressionable young children."

Ed stared around the other members.

Matthew Johnstone stood. "I think it's best if you go."

"What are you doing?" Ed said.

"Protecting our village. It's a shame you don't feel the same way," Matthew replied.

Arthur had heard enough. He couldn't believe in this day and age he had to deal with this crap. "Ed, let's go."

But Ed hadn't finished. "You people make me sick. Well for the record, I can let you know that Arthur and I are a couple. Have been for weeks. I don't give a fuck what you think or say because I'm happy. Really properly happy. If that makes you uncomfortable, then so be it."

He went to join Arthur at the door, but stopped as he passed the bar. James stood stock-still. The look of revulsion on Ed's face made Arthur genuinely scared.

"I will never forgive you for this. Never." Ed spat the words at James as though they were bullets.

Before he had a chance to reply, Ed took Arthur's hand and they walked out of the pub. They didn't get very far. Arthur sank down on one of the benches. He felt too tired to cry. Ed sat next to him.

"Come on now. This is all my fault. I shouldn't have dragged you in there. I'm sorry."

"It isn't going to stop, is it?" Arthur said, weariness taking over him.

Ed rubbed his back. "Of course, it will. Listen to me. Villages are strange places. When change comes, it feels like the biggest deal in the world, but soon enough, people get used to it. Come on, let's get the van and go to Holton. I'll treat you to a pizza. Fuck the omelette."

Arthur shook his head sadly. "I think I want to go home. I need some time on my own."

They walked in silence through the village. By the time they'd turned the corner past Knott Wood and to Christine's cottage, Arthur just wanted to hide under the duvet from everything.

"Sure you don't want to come to the farm?" Ed asked hopefully.

"Ed, I really appreciate everything you said tonight. Especially the bit about us being a couple. But I'm the type that needs to lick his wounds alone. You understand that?"

Ed brought him in for a hug. "Of course, I do. If you change your mind, no matter what time, I'll leave the door on the latch. Let's face it, my shit guard dog won't stop you."

Arthur gave Ed a kiss. He let himself in through the garden gate, knowing Ed would be watching him.

The house lay silent when he got in, then he remembered that Christine had choir practice. Byron weaved through his legs. Arthur knew he'd been fed but he gave him the rest of the can anyway. At least he could buy Byron's love.

He heated through some pasta Christine had left in the fridge. As he ate, he dialled his friend, Lincoln, back home.

"Well, hello there, Mr Countryside."

Just hearing his voice and the connection to home, Arthur burst into floods of tears. It took him a while to calm down before he explained everything that had been happening.

"Are you fucking kidding me?" Lincoln said eventually. "What a backward bloody place it sounds. How many more weeks have you got?"

Arthur hiccupped. "Four. But that's not the point. I like it here, apart from that bitch."

Lincoln laughed. "How can you? Okay, you thought you needed it after Martin, but you've always gone way overboard, love. Three months' rehab after a summer of partying? You're hardly *Trainspotting* material."

Lincoln had tried his best to persuade him not to go. He had totally ignored how low Arthur had been, blaming it all on the break-up.

"How are you anyway?" Arthur said, feeling guilty. He hadn't been in touch with anyone since he'd been here except for his mum and dad.

"Had a great night last weekend. The season has started and there's plenty of totty."

Arthur forced a laugh out.

"Come home, babe," Lincoln continued. "You can stay with me instead of the olds. We can get you past all this."

Arthur thought about Ed. They had only really been together a few weeks, but he did have strong feelings for him. If he just walked away to his old life, would he always wonder what would have happened if he'd stayed? How could he repay Ed for that speech in the pub by bailing out? "I'll stick it out until the end of term. See how the land lies."

"Ooh what a wonderful martyr you are," Lincoln exclaimed. "Well make sure you come home before Connie's birthday. Word is the Funny Girls are performing. You love them."

Arthur couldn't deny he loved the drag icons of Blackpool. Perhaps he could even take Ed. "I'll call you."

He finished the call and made his way upstairs. He desperately wanted to sleep. Instead, he lay for hours mulling things over, all the time the little bag in his sock drawer calling to him.

Eventually Christine came home. She called to him, but he pretended to be asleep. The television went on and he listened to her watching the late news. Then she went to bed and the house fell into silence again.

He couldn't stand it anymore. He leapt up and rifled through his drawer, finding the bag that had been taunting him. He grabbed a mirror and made himself a generous line. With a shaking hand, he rolled up a ten-pound note from his wallet and snorted up the powder. The drug hit him like a mini explosion. He exhaled. God, it felt good.

The euphoria didn't last long. He looked at himself in the mirror and felt such loathing. All that work at getting over this crap and he'd let it take a hold at the first sign of trouble. A rage started to build in him. It didn't help when he thought about James. How could he stand there and let his sister have a meeting to run a gay man out of their village? The hypocrisy made Arthur want to be sick.

The church clock chimed eleven. Last orders.

He absolutely would not go down without a fight, no matter what Liz or Lincoln or Matthew bloody Johnstone said. Knowing sleep was a long way away and against his better judgement, he needed to act decisively. A plan formed and he threw on a fleece.

Doing his best not to wake Christine, he crept down the stairs. It reminded him of sneaking out of his parents to go to the gay bars of Blackpool. Once out on the road, the fresh air hit him like a mallet. Somewhere a sheep called to another. Did they never sleep?

Arthur pulled his shirt closed and marched towards the green. He didn't care if anyone saw him. He would not behave like a criminal. The lights were still on in the pub, and Arthur peered through the window. There were no customers, but James was still clearing glasses. There was no sign of Becky.

He went to the door he had run out of only hours before, but this time he knocked hard. He had things on his mind, and he would get them out.

"We're closed," James said from inside.

Arthur knocked again. He heard grumbling then a key in the door.

"Didn't you hear me? We're —" He stopped in his tracks when he saw him on the front step.

Arthur pushed past him into the pub. "I thought we should have a word."

James shut the door behind him. "I don't want any more bloody trouble."

"No, me neither, but I seem to have a shitload of it."

James sighed. "Come on. I'll get you a drink."

"Anything but local gin."

James went behind the bar. "Ouch. But I guess I deserve that."

He poured Arthur a glass of wine and one for himself. "Go on, then," James said. "Lay into me. Tell me how awful you think I am."

"My feelings about you aren't important. How can you do this and look at yourself in the mirror?"

James sighed. "Because I have to. It's hard in this village sometimes and everyone comes here for comfort. I can't take sides."

"You can't take sides? You were in a relationship with Ed for seven years. You and I went to bed right above where we're sat. You've already taken sides, James, you fucking hypocrite."

James rubbed his face. "She's my sister. What am I supposed to do?"

"Perhaps I should give her something a bit meatier to worry about than her kid's teacher. What if she knew her own brother was one of the perverted damned as well?" Arthur instantly regretted saying it. The coke made him nasty, everyone said it. Why had he given in?

"Please don't do that, Arthur. If you want me to beg you, I will. I lost Ed because of this. I can't lose my business. I will do what I can. I promise you that. Please, Arthur."

Arthur rubbed his eyes. This had been another mistake driven by anger. He drained his glass and got up to leave.

James stood, barring his way. "Arthur. You have to tell me you won't."

"Get out of my way." Arthur went to barge past him but James' strong hands on his arms held him in place.

"Arthur."

He needed to get out of there. "Of course, I won't tell her."

James' whole body relaxed. "Thank you. I will stop her. Fuck knows how. Once Liz has something in her head, it's easier to stop a jumbo jet."

"This isn't fair," Arthur said.

Before he knew it, they were kissing. James wrapped his arms around him, the strength of him so reassuring. Suddenly reality hit and Arthur leapt from James as if scolded. "I can't do that. Things are complicated enough."

James hung his head in shame. "I can't stop thinking about you. I feel like shit admitting it but it's true."

Arthur felt winded. "What are you playing at? Are you trying to ruin things for us?"

James sank down on a bar stool. "Of course not. I just…I think about you, that night."

He couldn't listen to this. He quickly made his way to the door. Confusion and anger fought for supremacy inside him.

"Arthur. I will stop her," James said.

Arthur didn't know what else to say. He just nodded and set off back to his bed where a sleepless night awaited him.

Chapter Thirteen

James skimmed the stone, but it plopped into the tarn after the second bounce. Frowning, he picked up another and it did the same.

"You always were rubbish at this."

Liz picked up a stone, examined it carefully then launched it into the still water. It bounced about five times before disappearing, leaving a ripple.

They wandered along the shore for a bit.

"I don't know. You ask me for a walk and haven't said more than five words," Liz complained.

"You know why I want to talk to you."

Liz sighed. A heron took off from over the other side of the water. "I know. Is it whether I'm entering the baking competition at the fête? Or maybe you want a hint on what I've got you for your birthday? Or perhaps it's bloody Ed."

"Not just Ed, Arthur too."

Liz stared at him. He could see his mother's haughty expression in her face. She had never been one to argue with either.

"Why do you care about him? You don't even know him."

"Neither do you," James said, being very careful to keep his voice under control. "You don't believe half of what you're saying."

"Don't I?"

"No."

They walked in silence for a little while.

"Shall we go into Bennett's Woods, see if the tree is still there?"

They used to play down here all the time as kids. Their parents would be busy in the pub so they would climb over the fence in the car park and disappear into the woods.

Liz followed him into the trees. "I thought you'd be more concerned with your nephew's teacher. What kind of rubbish he might be filling his head with?"

James threw his hands up. "Liz, you were telling me what a good teacher he is. Now you've turned into some judgemental nineteen-fifties puritan. What are you doing?"

Liz stopped and stared at him. "I'm protecting the village."

"Oh bullshit. You're diverting attention from your bloody extension."

They started to walk again.

"You don't know what you're talking about," she muttered.

"I know you better than anyone on this planet."

They walked in silence.

"I couldn't stop it now even if I tried," she said eventually. "It's not just me who's upset."

"It's you holding meetings about it and going snooping on the internet. I'm telling you now, you won't have another meeting at the pub."

Liz raised an eyebrow. "The big man speaks. Dad would have let me."

"Dad hasn't been behind that bar for many years."

They reached the place where the tree they had played in as kids should be, but only a stump remained.

"Oh no," Liz said.

"I guess nothing lasts forever."

They stood looking at their old childhood friend, or what remained of it.

"Maybe I'll calm it down," Liz said, taking hold of his hand. "Would that make you happy?"

He squeezed her hand. Despite her many, many faults, he loved her furiously. "I think it would make everyone happy."

"Hello."

They both jumped at the voice. James' nerves jangled as Ed approached.

"I saw you two coming in here and I guessed where you'd be heading."

"It's gone," Liz said.

Ed stopped in his tracks and surveyed the stump. "Oh," he said, glancing at them. "When did that happen?"

"God knows," James said sadly. "I haven't been in here for donkey's years."

How many picnics had they had in the branches of the tree? Liz and James had pinched from the kitchens at the pub and Ed had broken into his mum's baking tin. They would play all day in the holidays in their own little kingdom.

"How are you two doing?" Ed asked.

"We're doing okay," James said. The atmosphere felt positively sub-zero. "How are you?"

Ed glanced at Liz. "I've been better."

She scowled, the moment smashed like ice. "And I suppose that's my fault?"

Sighing, Ed sat on a tree stump. "What do you want me to say, Liz? No, it's not your fault that the man I am fast falling in love with cries himself to sleep at night? I can't do that."

James battled the tears that were threatening to spill out of him. The thought that Ed could be in love with someone other than him burnt him like a raging fire. He glanced at Liz to make sure she couldn't read his face. He needn't have worried. Liz had other things on her mind.

"Falling in love?" she spat, pulling her arm free from James. "What a load of shit. Do you think we wouldn't have known you were gay by now?"

"Some things can be right under your nose, and you don't see them," Ed returned, pointedly staring at James.

James panicked that Liz would pick up on his not-so-subtle behaviour, but he had nothing to worry about. She had gone straight into full flow.

"I don't care what you get up to in the privacy of your own home, Ed Cropper. But when it starts to affect my child, then I have something to say."

James threw his head up to the heavens. Just as he had started to make progress, Ed had undone everything.

"I hope you're having a good year at that farm of yours," she continued. "Because you'll be supporting this man you love before very long. That's if I have anything to do with it."

She didn't wait for a response and stormed away from the two of them.

"I hope you can sleep at night, you miserable cow," Ed shouted after her.

James plonked himself down on the stump next to Ed. "Nice one," he said, rubbing the top of his nose. A tension headache spread across his whole head and he didn't need that on top of everything else.

"What? Am I supposed to just let her get away with it?"

"No but before you came thundering through the undergrowth, I'd got her to agree to calling it off."

Ed's mouth opened and closed. He frowned. "Shit."

"Yes, shit."

They sat in silence for a little while, listening to the wind rushing through the branches.

"We used to have fun down here, didn't we? The three of us," Ed said.

"I seem to remember us having a bit more fun once Liz stopped coming."

It wasn't too far from here that they had had their first kiss all those years ago. They had pinched some booze from the pub and one of them had suggested they practise kissing on each other. They had freaked out at how good it had been and hadn't spoken about it for a good seven years. Then one night in the pub, after James' parents had been killed and six months after Ed's had died, they'd found each other.

Ed reached across and took his hand. It still felt electric when he touched him. "I miss you," he said.

"You seem to be doing all right. You're so much stronger than I've ever known you."

"We've made a right mess of things, haven't we?"

James knew there was no "we" in it. He had made a mess of things. "I took you for granted. I'll never not regret it but I'm glad you're happy. You know, with Arthur."

Ed pulled his hand away and ran it through his hair. Something scurried in the undergrowth nearby but other than that silence reigned. "Happy? How can I be happy when I never see you? We've spent nearly every day together since we were bloody born."

James hadn't expected this. "I thought you hated me."

Ed laughed. "I love you, you dick. I can't turn that off because you annoy me."

They sat in more silence, the confession lingering like an awkward guest at a party.

"I love you too," James said. "I wish I'd been braver. Is there a chance we could — "

Ed got up. The moment snapped like the twig under his boot. "I'm sorry. I can't do that to Arthur. He's got more than enough on his plate because of us."

James stood too. Suddenly, he wanted to be anywhere but in this wood.

"No, of course not. He's a good guy. He doesn't deserve any of this."

"I wish I could split myself in two. I reckon that's the only way I'd ever be happy."

James put his hands on the tops of Ed's arms. "You'll be happy. You're the type. I'm just gutted I wasn't the one to make it happen. Arthur is a lucky guy."

They stared into each other's eyes for a second then, like an unspoken agreement, set off in opposite directions.

* * * *

James drifted through the rest of the day feeling so angry with himself. Three months ago, everything had been great, and now he could be losing everyone who meant something to him.

By the time he got to rugby practice that night, he needed to work off the tight ball of energy that had taken up lodging inside his chest.

Andrew Norris faced him, built like a solid wall of muscle. Andrew had only recently joined the team, coming to the village from Newcastle. James focused.

"Right, lads," Rob Holdsworth shouted. "The one who gets the other down owes him a pint."

He blew his whistle. The hard muscular body slammed into him. He tried to writhe himself free so he could get a better grip, but Andrew grappled around his waist. Grunting, each tried to best the other. In the end, James managed to get the upper hand and floored Andrew into the ground.

He stood and held out his hand to help him up. "You're on a mission today, mate," Andrew said, panting. "Remind me not to get on the wrong side of you."

"Okay, those who were floored. Let's have a circuit of the pitch."

Andrew made a face. "Thanks a bunch. Plus, I owe you a pint."

James shrugged. "All in a day's work."

"Remind me to give you my number later," Andrew said with a wink. "I never fail to pay my debts."

James couldn't help but grin. "I own the pub. I'm not difficult to find."

"Not the same though, is it? Give me a shout when you get a night off."

With that he set off with the other players. Rob walked over to James and handed him a bottle of water, which he glugged down.

"Want to talk about it?" Rob asked.

"Nothing to talk about. I just had that winner's hunger today. Nothing more to it than that. I thought you would be pleased after the pasting we got last season."

Rob held his hands up. "Me and Jenny are worried about you."

James looked towards the school. Life had been a lot easier in the days when they'd all kicked a ball against the wall and swapped football stickers. "I've got a lot on at the moment. Nothing major."

"Liz?"

"You heard then."

"Everything goes through Jenny's surgery. What is she doing to that poor lad?"

James did not want to have this conversation. He knew his friends were blaming him for it when they had no idea what they were talking about. "You know Liz. There's nothing I can do to stop her."

"You sure about that?"

James frowned. "Yes, I'm sure about that. He'd be better off going somewhere else and letting things get back to normal."

Rob looked at him in a way that made him uncomfortable. "And what about Ed?"

There went that familiar tingle, deep down inside, whenever his name cropped up. He had enjoyed seeing him that afternoon so much. Even under these circumstances. "He decided to be gay pretty quickly. No doubt he can decide if he wants to follow his lover or not."

Rob sighed and stared out at the rugby pitch. "You can get mad if you like but Ed hasn't just decided he's gay, has he?"

He might as well have shot James at point-blank range. His head swam. "What are you on about?"

"James, come on. Do you think the whole village doesn't really know about you two? I bet even Liz does, deep down, if she stopped for one minute to think."

James gripped the railing, unsure what to say.

"I'm not trying to upset you," Rob continued. "I'm trying to say that most people don't care. Of course, Liz has whipped up a few of the rotten apples to support her, but most of them are doing it so they don't have to drive ten miles to the bloody supermarket."

"I don't know what to say."

"Don't say anything to me, you big ape," Rob exclaimed. "Say it to the people who bloody matter."

The rest of the players had returned, panting. Andrew found his way to James' side.

"I'll pay you back for that." He laughed.

Rob clapped his hands together. "Right, that's it for tonight. It's too bloody hot. If anyone wants to get their pints in, I'm sure James here will be glad of the business."

The sweating men started to move towards the car park.

"Maybe I'll see you down the pub later?" Andrew said.

"Yeah, I'll be there," James replied.

Andrew set off to his car. Rob clapped him on the shoulder.

"What?"

"You're not that bloody thick, are you?"

James watched Andrew walking away. Had he been hitting on him? He'd never thought about being with anyone other than Ed. Arthur had been different. It had just sort of happened but actually going on a date with someone?

"Life is too bloody complicated at the moment to make it any worse."

He walked off to the pub more confused than ever. Andrew ticked all the boxes, but the spark James had had with Ed and Arthur wasn't there. But they had found each other, leaving him where? He would give anything to speak to Ed about this. It felt like in a few short weeks he had lost everything.

.

Chapter Fourteen

Arthur made it to the end of the week with no other run-ins with Liz, thankfully. He couldn't stop thinking about what James had said, but when he did, guilt overran him. Christine had invited Ed over for a board games night. Madge wholeheartedly approved of this as she lay on the rug munching into some delicacies Christine had got for her. A highly unimpressed Byron scowled from his vantage point on the back of Christine's chair.

They were sitting around her dining table, setting up a game of Scrabble when Christine sighed loudly.

"You always sigh when you have something bad to tell me," Arthur said, reaching for his glass as though it were a shield.

"I didn't know whether to leave this until Monday morning, but I can't. Listen, Arthur, a petition was handed in at home time. Yes, from Liz. It has about twenty signatures on, signatures that I will be checking the validity of."

Arthur glanced at Ed, who had started to tremble with rage. "A petition? What for?" he asked Christine.

"I don't think I have to spell it out, do I? I told you the other day, you are protected by the law. But they are threatening to take their children to Holton. Stupid narrow-minded people."

Ed reached across and took Arthur's hand. "She's right, love."

Arthur got up and with a shaking hand took the bottle of wine from the sideboard. He almost spilled it over the table as he refilled his glass. "This is a tiny school, Ed. We have about fifty pupils. We can't afford to lose any. They'll close us."

Christine took the bottle from Arthur and filled her and Ed's glasses. "It won't come to that. She wouldn't dare. God knows how many generations have gone to that school."

Ed squeezed Arthur's hand. "James will stop her. I know he will. He promised me."

Arthur moved his hand away. "When did you see James?"

"Oh, we need another bottle." Christine scurried into the kitchen.

"When did you see him?" Arthur repeated.

"A few days ago. We bumped into each other in the woods. He was with Liz. I tried to talk to her, but she wasn't for talking and buggered off to her lair. I tried to get across to James that he's the best person to help here. He's a good man, Arthur, honest he is."

"Well, you would know, I guess," Arthur said, taking a slug of wine.

"Yes, actually I would know."

Arthur stood, causing the board to fall to the floor and tiles to spill everywhere. "I'm an outsider here, whichever way you look at it. I just don't know if I have the strength for it. I think it's best if you go home, Ed. I need to think."

Ed seemed about to argue but then just nodded. "Come on, Madge."

She sloped off. The door banging cut through Arthur. Christine came in, looking worried.

"There wasn't any need to ask Ed to go," she said, sitting down.

The walls of the small front parlour seemed to close in on him. But he didn't dare go out for a walk, in case he bumped into someone who just wanted another argument.

"I do everything wrong, don't I?" He couldn't bring himself to look at her. He had brought trouble to her door, which had been his last intention.

"I didn't say that. I just thought we should discuss it like adults."

Finally, Arthur met her gaze. "Can't you see it? He's obviously still in love with James. I'm just a bit of fun until that sorts itself out."

"I should have known. James Durkin and Ed Cropper? They managed to keep it quiet, even from me."

"Seems as though they can lie to anyone if they put their minds to it."

"Arthur, I've known those two since they were tiny. Ed Cropper being able to lie and use someone? Never in a month of Sundays." She scrutinised him. "There's more yet, isn't there?"

He nodded. "James and I. We…well, we've had a couple of encounters."

She whistled. "You really have got yourself caught in the midst, haven't you? Then all this business with Liz. Poor James must have not known what to do. Does Ed know about you and James?"

"He knows about the first time, but not the second. We only kissed. I couldn't help myself. Every time I see him, I don't think about him and Ed—I think about him and me. But I feel strongly for Ed too. It's all such a mess."

When it all came out in the cold light of day, nobody escaped looking squeaky clean. Least of all him.

"You could have spoken to me. These lads need to be treated kindly, Arthur. They've been through so much. Everyone in the village knows that."

He couldn't bear to be judged as the villain on top of everything else. He wanted to be on his own. "As a stranger, I wouldn't have the first clue, would I? Everyone here knows what's going on and I'm just the idiot who bears the brunt of their ignorance."

He didn't wait for Christine to respond and stormed up to his room. A childish act but he couldn't help himself. He knew exactly what to do, and it filled him with revulsion. He went straight to his sock drawer and pulled out the little bag he still hadn't been able to throw away.

He poured some of the powder out on a book and ripped some of the cover off to make a line. Searching around, he found a piece of paper from a pad and rolled it up. He needed the hit more than anything. Just as he went to snort it, the door opened.

"Arthur, I think we should...."

Christine stopped dead in her tracks. The horror on her face made him want to throw up. "What in God's name do you think you're doing?"

He straightened up. He couldn't possibly defend himself. "I..."

"Drugs? In my house? Give them to me now."

With a shaking hand, he picked up the book and gave it to her. "I don't know what to say. Christine I'm so sorry. It's just with all this—"

"No. You will not use this as an excuse. You have five minutes to get yourself together then come downstairs. We need to talk about this properly."

She left the room, slamming the door in the process. Arthur sank on the bed. Adrenalin threatened to overtake his whole body. He stared around the lovely room Christine had given over to him. He remembered his first night here, feeling so positive and that he had turned his life around. It had only taken a few weeks for that to come crashing in on top of him.

He had to face her although every pore of him wanted to run out of the door and never stop. He owed her more than though so with a heavy heart, he went down the stairs and into the lounge.

She sat in her chair, Byron on her knee. "Sit down." She motioned towards the other chair.

He sank down, looking everywhere but at her. He didn't need to face her to know the stern expression he would be met with. "I'll go, tomorrow," he said eventually.

She sighed. "I would have defended you to the hilt. In fact, I had prepared the offer letter for you to be permanent next term."

It cut into his heart so deeply that he wanted to cry out. The tears ran down his face.

"I've let you down."

"Arthur, I cannot have someone in my life, professional or personal, who turns to drugs when the going gets tough. I know you were honest with me about your struggles, and I am fully aware it is an ongoing battle. But I am the headteacher of the school."

He knew he had put her in a terrible position.

"I still think you are one of the most gifted teachers I have ever met," she continued. "But events have taken over you. I think it's best if you do go, tonight. I will drive you to the station."

He slumped in the chair. He had ruined everything.

"But," she said, "I will keep that letter on file. I don't have to start recruiting until the middle of August. I want you to really think about your future over the next three weeks. Then contact me."

He couldn't believe she had thrown him a lifeline that he didn't deserve. "I don't think I'll be back," he said. "It's too hard. I just want to start again."

She stroked Byron, who purred his appreciation. "One day you will realise that running to new starts is not the way to beat your demons. I don't want you back unless you are one- hundred-percent committed, so if you don't feel that you can do it, then I will respect that decision."

He glanced at the clock. It was just coming up to seven. "Can I go and say goodbye to him first?"

She put her hand on his knee. "Of course, you can."

The tears carried on flowing as he walked up the farm track. His stomach lurched as Ed came out of the field that led onto the track. He also stopped, shocked. Madge bounded over to him and rubbed herself against his legs.

"What is it?" Ed said, his face a picture of worry.

"I'm leaving."

Ed ran over to him. "You can't," he said. "What about us?"

Arthur took his hands in his own. "You're a wonderful man, Ed, but let's face it, you're still in love with James. I can't fight him for you as well as fighting his sister for my career. It's too much."

Tears started to spill down Ed's face. "I won't deny that I love James. I probably always will. But I love you too. We could have more of a chance. Please, Arthur. Don't go."

Arthur let Ed's hands drop and leant down to scratch Madge behind the ears. "I have to. It might not be for good. Christine has said I can miss the last few days of school."

"But—"

Arthur silenced him with a kiss. He could smell the cologne on him that he'd bought. This time he didn't cry. Somehow, he drew on some superhuman strength that he didn't know he had. Ed was openly crying though, and it killed him to think he had caused those tears.

"Let me go, Ed. I would never make you choose. That's not my style. You're a wonderful man and I just hope James realises that pretty bloody soon."

Before Ed could make any more protest, Arthur turned and made his way down the farm track for the last time. He didn't turn once. He needed to get out of this toxic place as fast as his legs would carry him.

Chapter Fifteen

They were tucking into the sausage and chips as though they hadn't eaten in a year. James leant against the kitchen counter and sipped his coffee. He loved having his two nephews around the old table. It reminded him of when he and Ed would wolf down their tea before going out to play.

"Slow down there, you two. No one is going to steal it from you," he said.

Dean rolled his eyes while he munched on a chip. "Mum's on a health kick so we're only getting lentils and stuff. This is amazing."

It had been a long time since anyone had complimented the food in The King's Arms.

Joel spiked the sausage with his fork and bit the end off.

"Looks like you've lost your table manners, too. Cut that, please," James said, pushing Joel's hand so the sausage went back on the plate. He set about cutting the food with no argument. In fact, he hadn't cracked a smile since he had arrived. James sat next to him and rubbed his shoulder.

"What's up, champ? You're not your usual self."

Joel concentrated on cutting up his sausage and didn't say a word. James glanced at Dean for explanation.

"He's upset because his teacher has gone."

James frowned. "Art…Mr Whittaker? Where's he gone?"

Joel lifted a perfectly cut piece of sausage, dipped it in his tomato ketchup and popped it in his mouth. He chewed slowly and swallowed before announcing, "Mum has got rid of him."

Everything had been quiet on the Ed and Arthur front for a few days and things in the pub were picking up, so he hadn't had a chance to find out the current situation. He had hoped his sister had given up even after the spat with Ed.

"Mum threatened to take Joel out of school and got a few other mums to do the same with their kids," Dean explained.

To James' horror, a tear trickled down Joel's cheek and plopped onto his chips. With the dam firmly opened, he threw his cutlery down before bursting into tears. James wrapped his arms around his nephew as he sobbed.

"Perhaps he's just gone home early. He might be here next term," he said, rubbing his back.

"He won't," said the tiny voice buried in his chest. "It's not fair. I love Mr Whittaker. He shows us things so we can understand them." Joel stared up at James. "Did you know Rome was built by two brothers and their mum was a wolf?"

"No, I didn't know that," James said, stroking his nephew's hair.

"See, Mr Whittaker knows everything and now he's gone. We were going to do Vikings next term too."

The wailing continued and he hid his face again in James' now incredibly soggy jumper. "Is this true? He's gone."

Dean put his knife and fork down. "Yeah. He went at the weekend. Mrs Carrington is teaching all the kids for now until they can find someone else for September."

"She didn't even know Romans used a sponge on a stick to wipe their bums," came a forlorn voice.

James knew he should go to the farm and see Ed. As hard as it would be helping him nurse a broken heart, he had to try. After all, he had been part of all this.

The door opened and Liz came in. She stopped in her tracks when she saw the scene in front of her. "What's going on here? Joel, are you all right?"

Dean stood and came around to Joel. "Come on, kid," he said, extracting Joel from James' arms and taking his hand. "Let's go home. I'll beat you on the PlayStation."

Joel, still sobbing, took his brother's hand, pointedly ignoring Liz.

"Aren't you even going to say hello to your mother?" she asked.

Dean put his head down and led his brother out of the pub kitchen, slamming the door behind him. Liz sank down at the table and took a chip from Dean's abandoned plate.

"They have no respect," she muttered.

"Can you blame them?" James replied, swiping the plate from under her. He would be damned if he fed her after everything she had done recently.

Liz had the face of superiority she always wore when she knew she was in the wrong. She clearly had every intention of styling it out. "I was protecting my children. You would have no idea what that entails, thank you."

James slammed the two plates into the sink, making her jump. "You were using your children to get your own way and you know it."

Liz sniffed. "Whatever. They'll forget about Mr Whittaker soon enough. Anyway, I didn't come here to talk about your...unusual friends. How did it go at the closed meeting last night? Did they vote in favour of sending my planning application to the county council?"

He knew his sister could be selfish, but that she hadn't even batted an eyelid at ruining a young man's career made him so angry that he could barely keep control. "As that's the only thing you seem to give a shit about these days, you'll be pleased to know you got a three to two majority."

A glow of triumph crept over her face. "I can just imagine which two voted against me. Who cares? The county will pass it no problem. Councillor Jackson told me personally he would back me all the way. Took a few discounts, mind."

James thought back to his conversation with Rob. If he only had Liz left, did that mean very much? She had disappeared into a world of spite. Their parents would be ashamed.

He decided on a last roll of the dice. "Now you have your way will you give up this ridiculous vendetta and let Arthur come back next term? With no trouble?"

Liz stood up. "You know, you're so obsessed with this that people will start talking about you soon. Is that what you want? To turn this place into some sort of gay pub that no locals would set foot in? Dad would love that."

She had crossed the line, finally.

"Don't you dare bring Dad into this. They would be ashamed of you. I know that much."

She reared up, always ready for a fight. "Don't make me laugh. You've tried to be a watered-down version of Dad for donkey's years. It seems no one dares tell you, but you're failing miserably. Rugby, parish council, this place? You're pathetic."

The words hit him like a tidal wave. Even she had the decency to look shocked that she'd said them.

"You've turned into a nasty, bitter woman, Liz. Get out. I can't bear the sight of you."

He couldn't be held responsible for what he would do next if she stayed within his reach.

"James —"

"I said get out."

She opened her mouth to say something else but thought better of it and stalked past him, slamming the door behind her.

James sank down at the table and burst into tears.

"Are you all right?"

Becky stood in the doorway. He dried his eyes with his sleeve. "Yeah, course I am."

She crouched next to him and put her hand on his. "I couldn't help hearing that. To be honest, most of the pub heard it."

He shuddered. He hated the idea of their dirty washing being aired in public. "Great," he said with a hiccough.

She rubbed his arm. "I don't know what your sister is on with, but she's wrong you know. You're a decent man all on your own."

"Thanks, Beck."

"Why don't you take ten minutes? I've got you."

He nodded and she disappeared through to the pub. Looking around the kitchen, he could still see his mum chasing his dad off when he tried to steal one of her mince pies for the carol concert. Through in the bar, he could hear his father hosting the quiz night to uproarious applause or the time he'd hired a karaoke machine and thought he was Elvis reincarnated.

With a body as heavy as lead, he got up and walked out of the door. He turned towards the church yard, deep in thought. He soon found himself on the edge by the iron railings, with the perfect view of the rugby pitch where they trained.

The familiar headstone with the white roses that he had put there last week awaited him. He half expected Liz to be there but no doubt she would be ranting to Robert or taking it out on Dean.

He slumped down on the bench by the railings and read the headstone he knew off by heart.

He had tried his best to fill the void his parents had left in the village. It broke his heart that Joel would never know how they'd had lit the place up without even trying.

"I fucked it all up," he said.

The tears came thick and fast. Liz's words had hurt because they were true. He was just a watered-down version of his father. Even before his parents had passed away, he had tried to please him. It felt like an epiphany. He knew Liz had been trying to hurt him, but she might have done him the biggest favour of his life.

"I need to do it my way now, Dad."

He stared past the churchyard to the green and the pub. He knew what he had to do and finally he had the guts to do it.

Chapter Sixteen

About a mile or so up the road from James, Ed lay on the sofa, ignoring the television that blared out. Madge cuddled into the side of him. She had no idea why her dad had the blues, but she knew her place. He stroked her head, lost in thought.

"Why does everyone leave in the end?" he said.

He thought about the happy times he'd had in this room. Times with his parents, he and James discovering their love for each other and finally Arthur filling the place with laughter and a new outlook on life.

It always ended up with him on his own.

They both jumped at a knock at the door. He knew exactly who this would be. The gossip had finally reached The King's Arms and James would be coming to ease his guilt. Ed would not give him that kind of satisfaction. He ignored the repeated knocking.

A face appeared at the window. "Edward Cropper, open the door this instant."

He leapt off the couch and made his way through the kitchen with Madge in hot pursuit. "You were supposed to bark, useless dog," he muttered. He heaved the door open and instantly felt about ten years old as the face in front of him frowned.

"Don't you dare ignore my knocking, young man," Christine said as she pushed past him and into the kitchen. She stopped to stroke Madge, who lapped up the attention from this new visitor. Christine sat down at the table and looked at him expectantly.

"Can I get you a drink, Mrs Carrington?" he said.

"That you can, lad." She glanced at the open bottle on the table. "I'll have some of that whiskey you seem to be tearing through."

He sighed and poured them both a measure, setting hers down in front of her before sinking into a chair opposite.

"What can I do for you?" he said.

"I came to see how you are. I don't suppose I'm the only one who is upset by all this."

Ed took a sip of the drink, the liquid burning his throat and the tears threatening to sting his eyes. "I can't focus on anything truth be told. I hate this bloody village."

Christine took a healthy swig and contemplated him. "No, you don't. You love it. But you love him too and that's perfectly fine. I've not seen you laugh like you do with him for many a year. I had a good talk with Arthur before he went. There was me thinking you had found love for the first time. I couldn't have been more wrong."

Ed couldn't give two figs about protecting James' ridiculous need for secrecy anymore. He just nodded.

"Two boys who did everything together. You always did have a special friendship. I should have known it would blossom into more. I'm losing my touch."

The tears were out of control now and Ed released them with a vengeance. "I don't know what to do, Mrs Carrington. I love them both so much and now I've lost them. I can't handle this. It's too much."

Christine reached across and took his hand. "Arthur told me something else and he begged me not to tell you but I'm going to."

Ed wiped his nose and blinked. What could she be about to tell him?

"Arthur and James. There is more to that than just two feuding exes of yours."

Ed frowned.

"Now before you fly off the deep end, they aren't having an affair or anything. But only because they both love you so much. Arthur told me they kissed. The night of the meeting at the pub. He went round to have it out with James and it just sort of happened."

Ed couldn't understand why Arthur hadn't told him himself. "So, you're saying they're in love with each other?"

Christine took another sip of her drink, clearly thinking hard about what to say next. "I wouldn't say they are in love yet. But I think they could be."

Typical. Ed would be left out in the cold again. "I don't know what's wrong with me. Why can't anyone love me?" he said.

Christine banged her hand down on the table in the same way she used to do on his school desk when he stared out of the window, daydreaming. "Oh, you silly little fool, haven't you listened to a word I said? You have two men madly in love with you, if you would only see it. They just happen to be very much attracted to each other too."

"I don't know what you're saying."

Christine drained her glass. "Firstly, I'll have another one of those. Then we'll have a chat about how relationships are like snowflakes, never two the same. There is a lot of love between the three of you. I think it's time we found a way to let it blossom."

Christine stayed until the end of the bottle. They talked and talked. At least things were finally out in the open, even if it meant that Arthur had gone.

Ed walked her back down the road to her cottage. "Thank you for coming, Mrs Carrington."

She rested her arm on his. "I think we're both old enough for you to call me Christine, don't you?"

In the distance the clock struck eleven. She squeezed his arm. "The pub will be empty by now, I should think." With a knowing wink, she let herself through her gate before turning to him. "Just go for it. You have nothing to lose and everything to gain."

He just nodded and set off into the village. Queen Street lay silent. He scowled up at Liz's bedroom window above the shop. She would keep for another day. Turning the corner, he could see James tidying up the bar through the small windows. With his heartrate at an alarming pace, he crossed the green and marched up to the door.

The colour drained from James' face when Ed came in. "Okay, Becky. I think I can take it from here. Why don't you get off home?"

"You sure?" Becky said.

"Yeah, off you go."

With one last look at the two of them, Becky disappeared into the kitchen. James and Ed could only stare at each other until they heard the door go. They launched towards each other, their mouths meeting with force.

Ed pushed his tongue into James' willing mouth and grabbed the back of his head. He wanted to feel as though nothing would divide them again.

James pawed at Ed's jacket, letting it fall to the floor of the bar. Ed followed suit, staring at James as he pulled the buttons open on his shirt. He ran his hands inside, feeling the familiar hairy chest waiting for him. God, he had missed this. His cock strained at his trousers as he took James' shirt off, letting it join his coat on the floor.

James dragged Ed's jumper and T-shirt off him. He needed to feel his skin on him. Ed couldn't bear not being connected to him.

They came up for air again.

"Someone might see us," Ed whispered.

"Come on," James said, grabbing Ed's hand and pulling him upstairs.

Once they got into his flat, they scrambled out of the rest of their clothes and James reached down and took hold of Ed's hard cock. Ed kissed his neck. He bucked his hips, fucking James' hand. "Oh God, I've missed you," he murmured.

"Then show me."

Ed dropped to his knees. James leant on the ladder, jutting out his hips. Ed licked the throbbing vein on his cock, looking up at him for a second before taking it into his mouth. James gripped the rungs as Ed sucked. Ed grabbed James' ass cheeks and controlled him, pushing him in and out of his mouth.

James' moans made Ed's cock harder, made him slide his lips up and down James' shaft faster.

James withdrew and put his foot on Ed's chest. He gently pushed him down to the floor, then lowered himself onto Ed's face, running his heavy balls across his mouth. Ed responded by licking at them, knowing this drove James wild. Judging by the moans coming from above, he was doing everything right.

James flipped onto all fours and guided his cock into Ed's mouth. Ed reached for his own cock as James fucked his mouth.

They shifted position, James on top of him. To feel his weight on him again made Ed want to cry. Ed wrapped his arms around the strong shoulders he had found safety in all these years as James ran his hands through Ed's hair.

"You feel so good," James whispered in his ear.

Ed entwined his legs around James' waist and rolled him over on the carpet amidst all the clothes. James slapped his arse hard, never once breaking the kiss.

Straddling him, Ed leant back. James knew what he wanted. "You know where they are," he said.

Ed crawled up the ladder to James' sleeping area. He rifled through the drawers by the bed and found the condoms and lube. With his legs dangling over the edge, he held them up for James. An eager James followed him up the ladder. Ed sank onto the bed, spreading his legs so James could find his place between them.

He ripped the condom wrapper open. James bent down and sucked hard at his cock, and Ed could barely focus as he pumped James' mouth furiously. "Fuck me, please, James," he moaned.

James took the condom from him. He slid it on his hard cock and let Ed pour lube onto his fingertips. Ed settled on the pillow as James smeared the cold liquid onto his hole. He inhaled sharply as James pushed a finger inside him. "Oh God, yeah."

James rubbed over his prostate, sending little bolts of electricity through Ed's body. He spread his legs wider, wanting to give James everything. James soon had two fingers inside him, and him rubbing against Ed's prostate sent shockwaves up Ed's spine.

Ed couldn't wait much longer and James knew it. He positioned himself so his cock pressed against James' hole. Gently he pushed the tip against him. Ed let out a cry as James found his way inside. Slowly, inch by inch, he buried his cock deep into Ed.

He held himself still for a second as Ed got used to it. Ed nodded and James started to rock back and forth. Each movement sent Ed into spasms of pleasure. It had been so long since he had had this fire and he needed more.

He rested his hands on James' knees, wanting every part of them to touch as James started to fuck him.

"God, I need this, James. Harder, please."

James took the hint and started to pound him. He bit at Ed's calf that rested on his shoulder then kissed him. Nothing could have felt more perfect than the weight of James on top of him while his cock filled his hole.

Leaning back, James closed his eyes, the sign he was going to come. Ed reached down and started to pull at his own cock furiously. "Oh God, James, I'm going to—"

He came in thick spurts, shooting up James' body. After the last aftershock left him, James let go and came with a cry, filling the condom with each buck of his hips.

James collapsed onto the bed next to Ed, both of them panting.

"Fucking hell," James said first.

Ed rolled into his outstretched arm and kissed him. James nuzzled into him. "You smell nice," he said. "Since when did you wear aftershave?"

"Arthur bought it for me."

James moved away, pulling the condom off and throwing it in the bin. He perched on the end of the bed. Ed frowned and sat up. This hadn't been the ending he'd expected.

"So, you returned to the old faithful, did you?" James said.

"What do you mean by that?"

"Your new man has done a runner, so you had to retrace your steps."

Ed couldn't believe this. Did James really think he was like that? "It's not as easy as all that. I've never stopped loving you. Not for one second. I just love him too. It's such a fucking mess."

James ran his hand across his head. "I have to tell you something."

"I already know."

James stopped and stared. "About me and Arthur kissing the other night?"

"Yes. He told Christine."

"Why didn't he just tell Liz? He could easily have shut her down if he'd told her about me."

Ed reached across and took James' hands in his. "He's a better man than that."

"You're right. I don't know. If I hadn't been so hung up on you, I might have beaten you to the post with him," James said with a laugh.

Ed kissed him. "What if there wasn't any competition? What if we made sure we were all happy?"

James reared back, shocked. "I'm listening."

A wry smile crept across Ed's face. "How about we really set the tongues wagging in Napthwaite? We could blow your sister's tiny little mind."

Chapter Seventeen

James loved feeling Ed's head in the crook of his arm, exactly where it should be. A grin crept across his face when he thought about the night before. It had felt good to be with him again, but they still had work to do before things could be perfect.

Ed murmured and lifted his head. His hair was mussed all over the place and he had that adorable foggy expression he always had first thing.

"Morning, handsome Eduardo," James said.

Ed scowled. "Don't start that again. What time is it?"

James glanced at his watch. "Nearly seven."

"I'd better get going. The cows won't feed themselves."

The morning chorus of birds had started in the woods behind, twittering away.

James ran his hand across Ed's chest. "You know how Jacob covered for you when we were on holiday?"

Ed frowned at this strange turn of conversation. "Yeah?"

"Can you get him to cover you for a couple of days? I'll ring Becky —"

Ed frowned. "We can't just stay in bed for two days, as tempting as that sounds."

James had been planning this for an hour. He sat up. "I say we go to Blackpool. Today."

Ed sat up too. "Are you being serious?"

"Completely," James said, kissing him. "We've pissed about enough. Let's do this properly."

Ed rubbed his eyes. James kissed him again. "I suppose if it all goes tits up, it can be an early birthday trip for you."

"Don't bloody remind me. Thirty-three. We're ancient."

Ed twisted him on the nipple. "Hardly."

James wriggled out of his grip. "Meet me at Mrs Carrington's in an hour. Now come on, scoot. We'll have to go today. If I'm not here to help Becky get ready for the fête, I won't see my birthday."

They scrambled down the steps and put their clothes on. Under normal circumstances, James would have relished sending Ed on his way with a spring in his step, but they had things to do.

Once Ed had gone, James cleared the bar that he'd left last night rather than face a major ear battering from Becky for leaving it in a mess, then rang her. It was still only eight-thirty and she wasn't known for being an early riser.

"What the fuck do you want at this time?"

"That is a charming way to greet your boss on such a beautiful summer's day."

"Tell me or I'm putting the phone down."

"Okay, okay." He laughed. "I have the deal of the century for you. If you can cover for me for a couple of days starting today —"

"It's my day off, arsehole."

"Listen. If you can cover for me for a couple of days starting today, I'll pay you double time. I will put all my efforts into finding a new chef. Plus, I will owe you three favours that you can claim at any time, including my working for most of the fête, allowing you plenty of time in the beer tent."

The silence on the other end of the line meant she could be persuaded. "Hmmm...you must be desperate. Throw in some free feeds when you finally get the food sorted and you've got yourself a deal."

"Done."

"Now piss off. I've got an hour before I have to be up."

The line went dead. Running upstairs to pack, he realised he had no idea what to wear to go on a mission to Blackpool, so opted for his jeans and figure-hugging T-shirt. At nearly thirty-three years old, he might be Jurassic compared to Arthur, but he wouldn't go down without a fight.

He drove to Christine's cottage. They would not be going anywhere in Ed's old Land Rover. To his dismay, he saw Ed walking down the road with Madge. "What are you doing?"

"Jacob's got pups. He'll do the farm but not the dog."

"We can hardly take her on a pub crawl around bloody Blackpool, can we?"

"I don't know, do I? Don't start getting stroppy."

They both put their hand on Christine's gate and James realised it was the first time they'd sniped at each other and not meant it in months.

"I bloody love you," James said and kissed him.

Ed could have been knocked down by a feather. "You won't kiss me in bloody Spain and now you're smooching on Mrs Carrington's doorstep?"

"The times they are a-changing," James replied as they walked down the path. He banged on the little cottage door.

"Hey, calm down," Ed said, taking hold of his hand. "You don't want her thinking we've come to blow her house down."

James grabbed Ed by the waist and kissed him again. "I'm not the big bad wolf unless you want me to be."

A wild-haired Christine answered the door in her dressing gown. "James? Ed? What on earth? It's eight o'clock...on a Sunday."

Ed glanced nervously at James. "Oh, I'm sorry, Mrs Carrington...Christine. We'll come back."

"Even Madge is here. It must be important. Get inside before anyone sees me looking like Medusa."

They followed her through to the kitchen.

"You two can make us a drink while I get changed. I will not speak to pupils in my nightgown, no matter how many years have passed since you were in my classroom."

In a matter of minutes, the smell of filter coffee filled Christine's kitchen and they all sat around her pine kitchen table.

"Right, that's better," she said, smoothing her wild curls. "So, what's the emergency?"

Ed started to speak, but James laid a hand on his, an action not lost on Christine who raised an eyebrow at them both.

"Let me," James said. "I've been a dick. I'm sorry, Mrs Carrington, but there's no other way of saying it. Ed told me about your conversation yesterday and you're absolutely right. Ed and I…well, we've made friends again. We tried to ring Arthur last night, but he isn't answering. We need you to help us. Please can you give us his address in Blackpool? Well, not his address. His parents'. You know what I mean. Sorry, I guess I'm nervous."

Christine sipped her coffee and took in their words. "Let me get this straight. You want me to give you the personal details of a colleague and a friend who is ignoring your other attempts at contact?"

James huffed, irritated. He had been sure she would help.

"How much do you pay Becky?" she continued.

"I can't tell you that," he replied, indignantly.

Christine threw her hands up. "There you go."

"This is totally different. We came here for your help. I'm surprised at you, I really am."

"Christine, you know how I feel about Arthur," Ed said, putting his hand on James' arm. "I feel the same way about James. You said yourself we all had a chance."

"If you won't tell us, then we'll just get in the car and try every door in Blackpool," James added for good measure.

Christine sighed. "You always were a dramatic one, James Durkin. I won't give you the address, but I will go to the fridge and find a bit of ham for that poor dog, who has been ever so patient. If you happened to glance at the mail I need to take to the postbox later...well, I can't very well do much about that."

She got up and opened the fridge, dramatically rifling around.

James grabbed the pile of letters on the side, and sure enough, there was one to Arthur. He quickly took a picture of it with his phone and replaced them.

"You can come out now," Ed piped up.

Christine gave Madge a few slices of ham which Madge inhaled. "And what is this young lady to do while you're tearing around the country?"

Ed glanced nervously at James. "She'll have to come with us."

Christine tickled her behind the ears. "We can do better than that. She can stay here with me. We'll have a fine old time, won't we?"

James leapt up and gave Christine a big kiss on the cheek. "I bloody love you, Mrs Carrington."

Christine allowed him to give her a hug. "I said to Ed yesterday and I'll say it to you. You can call me Christine now."

Ed hugged her on the other side.

She laughed. "Now off you go, the pair of you."

She shooed them out of the house, but not before Ed lavished Madge with cuddles. "You stay with Christine, you hear?"

By the time he got in the car, tears filled his eyes. "You're so soppy about that bloody dog," James said, ruffling Ed's hair.

Ed wiped his eyes. "She's the crappest farm dog in the whole of Yorkshire, but I do love her."

"And I love you."

They kissed again before James fired up the car and they sped out of Napthwaite.

The car journey felt strange. They couldn't talk about the uncertain future, so they settled on talking about the past.

James had missed being able to share this with Ed for these weeks. The thought that he could have lived his life without it seemed more than ridiculous now. It seemed impossible.

They arrived in Blackpool. Ed had booked them a hotel on the front from his phone, but they couldn't wait and the Sat-Nav took them straight to a semi-detached house in a nice little cul-de-sac.

James glanced at Ed. "Nervous?"

"Terrified," Ed replied.

They got out of the car and walked up the pristine garden path.

"Let me this time," Ed said, pushing in front of James. He knocked gingerly. A small woman with curly brown hair and glasses answered the door. She looked quizzically from one to the other.

"Mrs Whittaker?"

"Yes?"

"I'm sorry to turn up like this but my name is Ed Cropper and this is James Durkin. We're from Napthwaite."

To James' horror, her face crumpled into tears. "You'd better come in."

They followed her through the hallway. There were pictures of Arthur and what had to be his siblings on the wall. Mrs Whittaker dried her eyes and gestured for them to sit on the sofa.

A man who was the spitting image of Arthur came in and scanned the room. He frowned at his wife who dabbed at her eyes with a tissue. "Carol? What's going on?"

"They're the ones from Napthwaite," she managed.

Mr Whittaker sat down next to his wife and put his arm around her. James took in the room. It seemed like such a happy place with soft couches and French windows which led through to an immaculate garden.

"What do you want?" Mr Whittaker demanded.

James cleared his throat. "We came to see Arthur. He's had a bad time and we wanted to see if we could change that."

Mr Whittaker scowled at him. "Are you the landlord or the farmer?"

James should have realised Arthur had spoken to his parents about them. He glanced at Ed. "I'm the landlord."

"I'm the farmer," Ed said quietly.

"Well, I'm the father. A father who has barely had a wink of sleep since his son turned up on the doorstep. After we dried his tears, his bloody friends turned up and we haven't heard a thing since."

Mrs Whittaker burst into tears all over again.

"He's a fragile boy," she managed. "I'm just so worried."

"So what the hell do you want? You've used him as a plaything while you sort yourselves out. Surely you've done enough?" Mr Whittaker added.

"That's just it," Ed said, his voice shaking. "We haven't used him. Both of us got our feelings confused. If you could help us find him, we can sort this out. I promise you."

Mr Whittaker threw up his hands. "You must be bloody joking."

But Mrs Whittaker put her hand on his leg. "Gordon, wait a second. Let him speak."

She looked at Ed, willing him on. James let him speak. He knew he would put his foot in it if he even tried to contribute.

"We both had strong feelings for Arthur as well as each other. We believe that none of that should be wasted. If Arthur still feels the same way about us, we'd like to care for him together. To help him get over his problems. His job is still open."

Mr Whittaker seemed unconvinced. "And what about that bitch who's made his life a misery?"

James knew his cue when he heard it. "That bitch is my sister, and I was too busy trying to keep my secrets to do the right thing. You have my word, Mr Whittaker. Those days are past. My sister will pose absolutely no problem for Arthur again."

This seemed to impress the man in front of him. "You're going to risk your family, son?"

James puffed his chest out. "Family isn't always the people you're born with."

This set Mrs Whittaker off again. Her husband took her hand, but she nodded at him.

"Very well. But now I've met you, I'm telling you this. Hurt my boy again and I will make you wish you hadn't been born."

Deciding this was probably the best time to get out of there, James and Ed said their goodbyes and with a list of bars and addresses in their hands, set off to the town centre.

"Shit! Intense or what?" James managed. "His father is crackers."

"We deserved it," Ed said. "The whole time we were worrying about our needs, we pushed that poor lad backwards."

James reached across and took his hand. "We'll make it up to him."

They tried a couple of bars, all chrome and pumping dance music. No one had seen Arthur.

In the third one, a haughty barman cleaning glasses with a manky tea towel scowled at them. "Who wants to know?"

"You know him, then?" James said.

"I might," he replied.

James had no patience for this. The loud pop music battered his brain and after the drive and dealing with Arthur's parents, he wouldn't take the long road. "Don't piss us about."

The barman rolled his eyes. "I could have you thrown out, you know?"

James wasn't used to not being the one to call the shots in a bar and it didn't sit well with him. He'd be glad when he stood behind the bar of his own place again. He picked up one of the glasses the barman had been cleaning and held it to the light. As he'd suspected, muck streaked all over it. He swapped it for another and another.

"State of these. Wouldn't surprise me if the Environmental Health didn't shut you down on the spot if someone happened to give them a call." He squinted behind the bar. "The mess under those optics is weeks old and I dread to think what your beer lines are like." He turned to Ed. "A real health hazard, this place."

The barman stopped. "Fine, no skin off my nose. He was in last night with that skanky lot he used to hang around with. You'll probably find them in The Ship at this time. *Shopping.*"

James could imagine exactly what they would be buying.

If the bar they'd just been in had caused James concern, The Ship, a couple of streets back from the seafront, made him want to head for the hills immediately. A ramshackle building with a hanging basket full of dead plants swaying in the wind, it didn't scream homely hostelry. A gaunt man coughed violently by the door, smoking a cigarette.

"Oh Jesus," Ed said.

"Come on," James replied.

They ignored the vacant stare of the man as they went inside. A few ageless men in tracksuits were at the bar and at the rear of this grimy pub sat a group of better-dressed young people, amongst them, a tired-looking Arthur. His eyes widened when he saw them. "What the fuck are you doing here?"

"I could ask you the same question," Ed countered.

"He's minding his own business. Do the same," one of his friends piped up.

James wasn't going to stand for that. "Shut it, you," he said, drawing himself up to his full height. He turned to Arthur. "We need to talk."

"Is this them?" another of Arthur's friends asked.

Arthur nodded.

"Why don't you fuck off home to sheep-shit land where you came from? He's having a nice time with his real friends."

James would quite happily have cuffed both of these little queens on the ears, but he knew Ed would not approve.

Ed hadn't taken his gaze off Arthur, whose eyes didn't look right and who chewed at his lip furiously. "Arthur?"

"You heard him," Arthur said. "Fuck off back to sheep-shit land. I'm done with all of you."

A heavy-set pair of men came in the door. One of Arthur's friends nodded at them. They came and stood on either side of James and Ed. James didn't like the look of this.

"Buying again, lads?"

The mouthy one stood. "We would if we were given a bit of privacy, know what I mean?"

The guy next to James stared him in the eye. "You heard him. Fuck off."

James didn't fancy his chances against these two. He turned to Arthur. "We're at The Imperial. If you come to your senses."

Ed started to say something, but James took hold of his arm. "Come on. We've wasted our time."

"Arthur…" Ed said.

But Arthur looked away. This time Ed let James steer him out of the pub.

Chapter Eighteen

The phone vibrated against the bedside cabinet, the harsh sound cutting into his sleep. Ed opened his eyes. It vibrated again. James stuck his head above the duvet. "What the—"

Ed scrambled to the phone lighting up the room.

"It's one in the morning," James said.

Ed grabbed the phone and glanced at the display. Struggling with his hand-to-eye coordination, he managed to answer it. "Arthur?"

James sat up next to him in the bed then promptly dove under the covers when Ed turned the lamp on, flooding the room with light.

"Ed?" Arthur sobbed on the other end of the line.

"Are you okay? What's happening?"

"I'm downstairs. Please can I come up?"

Ed ran his hand through his hair. "Of course you can."

"They won't let me in unless you ring down."

"One second."

Ed reached across James to the phone by the bed. The faded glamour of the room meant it was one of those ones with a cord that got tangled and he nearly upended a glass of water as he pulled the handset to his ear and pressed zero.

James braved coming out from under the covers again, just to get the phone banging on his head as he got caught up in the flex.

"For fuck's sake," he said, giving up and getting out of the bed.

"Hello? Yes, can you allow my friend up, please?"

"He seems a little worse for wear, sir?" came the reply from the night manager.

"That's fine. Please just allow him."

"Very well."

The call ended and Arthur had terminated the connection on the mobile. James stood stark-naked looking very bewildered. He had never been a quick waker. "What the fuck is going on?"

Ed got out of bed and patted him on the arse. "He's coming up. You need to wake up."

They threw on their underwear and T-shirts. Butterflies swirled around Ed's stomach.

"Why am I shaking like a bloody leaf?" James said as if reading his mind.

"Listen," Ed said, taking his hand. "I think he's in a bit of a state."

James kissed him. "I'm a landlord, love. I can do people in states."

They were interrupted by a soft knock at the door. James went over and opened the door while Ed stood in the middle of the room.

A red-eyed and dishevelled Arthur stood there.

"You'd better come in," James said.

Unable to meet his gaze, Arthur came into the room. When he saw Ed standing there, he burst into tears. James and Ed both put their arms around either side of him.

"I'm sorry," Arthur sobbed miserably.

"Hey now," Ed soothed. "It's fine. We've all had a bad time." He finally had the two men in his life in his arms together, even though he had no idea of the purpose of Arthur's visit. He wasn't even sure Arthur did.

They finally untangled and Ed sat Arthur down on the bed. James poured him a glass of water.

"Your sister was right," Arthur said with a sigh. "I'm not fit to be around children."

James sat next to him. "Let's get one thing straight. My sister is never right...about anything."

Arthur couldn't help but laugh. Ed knelt between Arthur's legs. "What happened?"

"I couldn't get you two out of my head. The way I treated you and that you'd come all the way here. I had a big bust-up with my mates and they threw me out. I didn't have the guts to come here, so I've been walking."

Ed put his hand on Arthur's leg. "You don't have to be afraid of coming to us. Not ever."

Arthur glanced at James who had put his arm around him.

"My friends said you'd come to rub my nose in you being back together. Is that right?"

James hugged him tighter. "Not anywhere near right, you daft thing. We've got a lot to talk about, but I think that's for the morning. You need some sleep."

Arthur looked at Ed and stroked his hair. "I'm so tired."

Ed snapped to attention. "Come on. Out of those things and into that bed. There's plenty of room for three."

Arthur stood and started to take his clothes off, throwing them on the chair until he remained in just his white boxers.

"Who's going in the middle?" he asked, looking as though he could fall asleep standing up.

"You are, silly," Ed replied.

Arthur flung his arms around him while James got into bed. "I've missed you and it's only been a few days. I need to tell you—"

"All in good time." Ed guided him into the bed where James' arms waited. Ed had wondered if he would feel jealous seeing both the men he had feelings for together, but none of that mattered as Arthur nestled into the crook of James' neck.

Ed slid in behind him and cuddled into his back, laying his head on James' outstretched hand and taking hold of the other.

Arthur had already drifted off. Ed smiled at James. "Let's see what the morning brings then?"

James winked. "Never a dull moment these days. Goodnight, handsome."

Once he'd flicked off the lamp, Ed hadn't thought he would be able to get to sleep, but surprisingly he did drift off.

* * * *

The second time Ed woke in that old, dated hotel room, seagulls were cawing at the tops of their lungs. Arthur had moved in the night and snuggled into his side. James stuck his tongue out at him, his arm resting on Arthur.

Ed returned the gesture.

"Noisy bastards," James said.

Arthur opened his eyes. "The soundtrack to my bloody childhood."

They all giggled.

"Feeling better?" Ed asked, kissing Arthur's forehead.

"Ugh," Arthur said, scrambling so he sat against the pillow. "I reckon today will be a struggle, but I feel good being here."

James sat up too so all three of them were shoulder to shoulder.

"I guess we'd better have a chat," Ed said.

"Go on then, Captain Sensible," James replied, which made Arthur chuckle.

Ed reached across and flicked him on the bare arm. "Right, I'm just going to say it. We've been going about this all wrong. We've all had feelings for the other and I realised that we don't have to make a choice."

James turned to him. "You didn't realise it, to be fair. Christine did."

He could be so contrary sometimes that Ed could slap him, but he saw the glint in his eye and knew he was just trying to lighten the mood.

"Okay, Christine did."

"Oh God, Christine. She must hate me," Arthur said, shuddering.

James turned onto his side, resting his hand on Arthur's chest. "Don't be so silly. She wouldn't have kept your job open like that. She bloody loves you. It's easily done."

Arthur stared at him. "So, what are you both saying?"

Ed took a deep breath. "We're saying let's throw tradition out of the bloody window and see how we do it the three of us."

Arthur's head whipped around. "You mean…"

"Why not?"

Arthur stared up at the ceiling, lost in thought. "I suppose we could."

"Your mum thinks it's a good idea," James said.

"My mum? Do I even want to know?"

Ed quite liked listening to James winding someone up other than him. "We went there looking for you. Your dad doesn't think much of us, but I think he could be talked around."

Arthur seemed deep in thought. "I'll tell you who will hate this."

Ed and James caught each other's eyes before answering in unison, "Liz."

They all collapsed into fits of laughter.

James scrambled out of bed.

"Where are you going?" Arthur asked.

"Don't mind him," Ed said. "He has to shower as soon as he wakes up."

James disappeared into the bathroom.

"Are you really all right with this?" Arthur said. "I'm so sorry I treated you badly."

Ed snuggled into him. "Of course, I'm all right with this. Two men to love? What's not to like? As soon as Christine said it, all the pieces fell into place. I really think we should go for this."

"I'm up for it," Arthur replied.

Ed took hold of Arthur's hard cock. "I can see that."

Arthur wriggled out of his clutches. "Come on then. Let's seal the deal."

They padded through to the bathroom, shedding their underwear as they went. James' eyes widened when he saw them both come in.

"Time's up. We all need to get clean before we get dirty," Ed said.

James got out of the shower and made way for Arthur, who let the water run over his whole body. Ed kissed James before getting into the shower with Arthur. They soaped each other's bodies, all the while watching James enjoying the show. James was hard and stroking his dick. They had talked about threesomes before but Ed had never thought about it being with someone else they had feelings for. He wanted both of these men so badly his cock ached.

They quickly towelled themselves dry and went into the bedroom.

Arthur dropped to his knees. He started to kiss Ed's cock. Ed ran his hands through his hair.

James stood in the doorway watching, rubbing his cock.

Arthur leant below and licked Ed's balls, causing him to moan. As if he couldn't wait any longer, he took the whole of Ed's cock in his mouth. Ed held the sides of his head and began to pump.

Arthur turned to James. "You, okay?" he said, licking his lips.

Ed reached his arm out for him. He didn't look right, and Ed didn't want this to fail now they'd come so far.

"Yeah. I'm just a bit...well you know," James replied.

Arthur got to his feet and went over to him. He encircled his arms around his waist and kissed him. Ed walked behind him. He reached around James' body to play with his nipples and kissed the back of his neck.

"We've all done something together before," Arthur soothed. "There's nothing new in this room."

James grabbed Arthur's tight arse cheeks and their mouths found each other again. Ed nuzzled the back of James' neck, pushing his cock against him.

Ed dropped to his knees, spreading James' firm arse cheeks and delving his tongue inside. James shuddered.

Arthur knelt on the other side and instantly set to work sucking James' dick.

"Oh God yeah," James moaned, as they both worked on him.

With the ice seemingly broken, James soon squirmed free. "We might need a bigger bed." He laughed as he sank down onto the hotel mattress.

Ed and Arthur glanced at each other then crawled on top of him. Their limbs entangled as mouths found other mouths and hands found bodies.

Ed had no idea who he touched as they rolled around. He came up for air and found Arthur's cock. He sunk his mouth onto it, feeling him squirm with pleasure, then glanced up at James straddling Arthur's chest. Arthur's hands reached for his waist, guiding his cock into his mouth. Ed continued working on his cock, reaching to pull at his balls.

Seeing James' arse as he bent over Arthur's mouth presented too much temptation. He crawled up Arthur's body and dove his tongue between the cheeks again. His toned arse was incredible. Ed feasted on him as he continued to fuck Arthur's mouth.

Ed straddled Arthur's hard cock. He reached one finger down to James' hole and began to play with it.

Ed leapt off the bed and retrieved the condoms and lube they had bought at a petrol station in a fit of optimism.

Arthur and James had separated and Arthur sat up against the headboard. James knelt in the middle of the bed.

"Don't move," Ed said. "You both look so fucking perfect."

"And all for you," James replied.

"Come and show me what you're made of then," Arthur said, daring him.

Ed rolled the condom onto James' cock. He positioned himself between Arthur's legs and ran the lube over his hole. Ed lay next to Arthur, wrapping his arms around his waist. Ed kissed him as James pushed his cock against his hole. Arthur moved, letting him know he wanted more. James was only too happy to oblige, his cock pushing its way inside.

"Oh, fuck yeah," Arthur cried out.

James started to pump, slowly.

Arthur turned to Ed. "Give me your cock."

Ed got onto his knees, sliding his cock into Arthur's eager mouth. He reached down and tugged at Arthur's hard cock while kissing James.

James started to fuck him, pumping his dick in and out. Ed couldn't remember feeling this turned on in his life.

James stopped. "Your turn," he said to Ed.

James ran a condom onto Ed's cock and Arthur sat on top, guiding Ed's cock into him.

Arthur started to ride him, maddeningly slowly at first. James reached across and played with his cock. Ed grabbed James' cock, pulling at it as Arthur rode him hard. It wasn't going to take him long and he needed to come so badly. His head fell on the pillow as the familiar rush built inside him.

"I'm going to come," Ed cried. Arthur rode him faster and Ed started to moan. He came in hard spasms, pleasure flooding every part of his body.

Arthur moved away and lay beside a panting Ed. Arthur spread his legs. "Come on," he said to James.

James got onto the bed and dove his cock straight inside. Arthur rested his legs on James' shoulders.

"Show me what you're made of," Arthur said.

James started to fuck him.

Ed regained himself enough to kiss James before leaning down and kissing Arthur, running his hand down Arthur's tight torso and pulling at his cock.

Watching the two men fucking turned him on so much. Sweat was beading on James' forehead and Arthur grabbed hold of Ed's hand.

"Jesus, you're good," Arthur groaned.

"Oh God..." James managed. "I can't last any longer. I'm going to come."

Ed pulled furiously at Arthur's cock. As James threw his head back with a cry, Arthur came hard, his body a mass of convulsions.

James fell down on the other side of Arthur. Ed took the condoms off both him and James, throwing them into the bin. He snuggled into Arthur's outstretched arms.

"Good job we bought a value pack," James remarked.

"I'm not leaving this room until they're all used up," Arthur replied, kissing James' forehead then Ed's.

Ed knew they were probably waiting for a witty response, but he chose to lie there, listening to Arthur's heartbeat and feeling the afterglow of the best sex of his life.

Chapter Nineteen

"I don't see why it's a stupid idea," Ed exclaimed.

James winked at Arthur in the rear-view mirror. Arthur rubbed Ed's shoulder. "We need to go steady. We've only been together two days."

But what a two days it had been. They were coming home to the village after being holed up in the hotel room. He was aching in parts he hadn't realised could ache.

"Ed, we've been a couple for donkey's years and never lived together. Why on earth would we jump straight in now?"

"Besides," Arthur said, "I've missed Christine."

James grabbed his thigh. "But we will certainly make the most of things when we're there, Tiger."

He couldn't help but giggle. "Perhaps it would be a bit much for Madge. Oh, I can't wait to see her."

As they drove past the Napthwaite sign, anxiety crept into James' chest. Ed stroked the side of his face. "It'll be okay, you know."

He wasn't so sure about that, but he had to play along. Before he had to reply, he swung into the layby next to Christine's cottage. "Right, I'll see you later then."

Arthur planted his lips on James' cheek. "No matter what, you've got us."

Madge barked like crazy at Christine's window.

"And Miss Madge," Ed laughed, kissing him as well.

"Out, the pair of you."

"Soon will be." Arthur winked at him as they both scrambled out of the car.

The butterflies felt overwhelming as James drove into the village. Everyone seemed to be doing something. While they'd been away, a marquee had been put up on the green and bunting hung across Queen Street. He had loved the fête ever since being a kid. In those days they had done a fancy dress parade up and down the street. He and Ed had won one year as Buzz Lightyear and Woody. Obviously, he'd been Buzz Lightyear. They didn't do that anymore. Joel had informed him it wasn't cool in the slightest.

It was always especially exciting because his birthday fell around that time. What more could a kid ask for? He thought about his big day this year. Two men to spoil him. He just had one hurdle to get over before then.

"Morning, James." Mr Chan, a neighbour from across the road, waved at him.

"Morning. Mr C. Lovely morning."

The clouds were threatening.

"We're looking forward to the curry tonight, James. I hope you're planning on keeping those standards up," Mr Chan said encouragingly.

"Don't I always?" James laughed.

"Well, I haven't eaten at your place recently," Mr Chan said with a weak smile.

Nothing could get James down today. "Don't you worry. Mohinder is helping out. Then, yes, I will be employing a chef."

Mr Chan nodded.

That reminded him. He needed to get Mohinder's shopping list. He doubled back to head to the Post Office at the end of the street, where she lived with her son, Hardeep. Just as he turned the corner and picked up speed to try to get past Liz's shop without an interrogation, he bumped straight into Christine.

"Well, hello there," she said, smiling.

James couldn't wipe the beam off his face. "Good morning, Mrs C…Christine."

"I'm happy my lodger is home already."

"For the time being," James said with a wink. "They're at yours now. Tearful reunion between Ed and Madge."

Christine laid her hand on his arm. "I know the road ahead is going to be bumpy for you, James, but I just wanted to say I think you're doing the right thing."

James rested his hand over hers. "I wouldn't be doing anything if it wasn't for you. Thank you."

Just as Christine started to reply, Liz appeared out of the door. "There you are. I nearly called the police. Where the bloody hell have you been?" She noticed Christine's hand on James' arm and frowned.

"I'd better leave you to it," Christine said, not even turning to face Liz.

"Will you be coming later?" James asked.

"Try and stop me. I've been dieting all week."

Christine headed off down the road. Liz scowled after her. "Why was she touching you? She's weird, her."

James sighed. He wouldn't let Liz spoil his mood today. "I'd better go."

"Not so fast," Liz said, folding her arms. "Where have you been? Becky said you were taking some leave. You never take leave."

James started to move away. "I had a break. Bloody hell, Liz, it's allowed."

"Something's different about you." If Liz had a superpower, it would be X-ray vision. She could sense any deviation from the norm.

"Oh, for goodness' sake, stop mithering. I've got a million things to do before tonight. Will I see you later?"

"Of course. I want an update on my planning too."

James set off up the street without even replying. She would get an update this evening but not one she would be expecting. He and Becky worked hard all day getting the place ready. He wanted it to be immaculate. With the marquee across the road, inevitably the pub did a roaring trade. He popped his head around the door of the kitchen, which exuded the most delicious smells. They were a far cry from the usual heat-it-up meals he usually served.

"How are we doing, Mohinder?" he asked.

She replied with a flap of a tea towel and a huff. "Do you know where that son of mine is? He promised to come and help when he'd finished his round."

Hardeep, full-time postman and part-time kitchen hand, came through the door. "I'm here and don't think I can't hear you talking about me."

"About time," Mohinder said. "We'll be serving soon and you're late as usual."

James winked at Hardeep. "I'll leave you to it."

In the bar, Becky had done pretty much all the jobs. She had stocked the bar to the rafters.

"Are you expecting the zombie apocalypse?" he asked, shaking his head.

"I've set the room up," she said, ignoring him. "Are you going to tell me why you have an empty chair on either side of you? You're not that fat."

James scowled at her. "It's a surprise."

Becky shook her head. "Proper man of mystery these days, aren't you? Well, I suppose I'll get the mixers up from the cellar." She pushed past him and through the door that led to the cellar. James caught sight of his reflection in the mirror behind the bar and patted his stomach. He wasn't fat. Was he?

"Good evening, best night of the year incoming." Rob and Jenny Holdsworth came through the door.

"You're the first to arrive, so the first drink's on me. Don't tell anyone else," James said, scuttling behind the bar.

"A pint and a half please," Rob said.

"Sod that. If it's free, it's two pints." Jenny laughed with a wink.

James set about pulling the pints. Rob looked at him with interest and nodded at Jenny.

"What?" James asked, putting the first drink down.

"Oh, nothing," Jenny replied.

"I think someone sorted things out," Rob added.

James put the second drink down. "Stay tuned."

The next forty minutes passed in a blur as villager after villager spilled through the doors, sniffing the food-infused air and making various moans and groans, most of them about smelling decent food in The King's again.

The dining room had filled up nicely and the music blasted. The free wine had gone down rapidly.

"We should probably open another case of white," James decided.

"You're plotting something, I can tell," Becky said in a break from serving.

James pulled his best innocent face, which he knew would be fooling nobody. "Go and let Mohinder know we're ready. We can have ours later. I couldn't eat a thing anyway."

Becky flung her hands up. "Then why on earth did you make me do you a special bloody table with three seats on?"

James bundled her into the back. "You'll find out, Nosey Nora."

The service went flawlessly, and everyone tucked into the amazing food. James had been tempted, but every time he thought about it, nervous tension would stop him in his tracks.

He glanced at the clock. It was half seven. It was now or never. The door opened and all his nerves disappeared. James poured himself a glass of wine and marched into the dining room. The conversation died down as he took the table at the front of the room.

"Oh, here he is. Too posh to dine with us these days," Liz piped up.

A ripple of laughter fell around the room, but Napthwaite was like any village — people could sense when something was about to happen. The eager eyes staring at him told him he had their attention. Rob, Jenny and Christine were sharing a table. They smiled warmly at him.

He dithered for a second, nerves making his legs go numb.

"Come on, Mr Councillor," Liz shouted, oblivious to the change in mood. "Tell us why you've two chairs empty. Don't tell us you've got yourself two ladies. Never been able to land one and two come along?"

She had clearly been at the free wine. He could tell by the red rash creeping up her neck that he felt sure was replicated on his for very different reasons. They got this from their mother.

"Okay, first of all, I'd like to thank you for coming to the curry night. I trust you've had a good feed."

He took a swig from the wine.

"I've two pieces of business before we get stuck into the booze. As you know, I put this night on as chair of the parish council. I took on that role because I love this village and I made a commitment to you all that I would do what I thought was best for it. No matter what."

He stared directly at Liz.

"So, I'm going to announce that I've blocked the proposed extension for the mini mart."

Liz started to stand up, but Robert reached across to stop her.

"Family bonds aside, we all know it will destroy the feel of our special place and I couldn't have that on my conscience. Not for anyone. I'm sorry, Liz, I really am."

All eyes turned to Liz, who for once seemed at a loss for what to do. "You're a bloody snake, James. I'm not staying here to be humiliated like this." This time she got free of Robert and started to get her coat to leave.

"You might want to stay for the next bit. It concerns you more than most," James said. He knew that the gossip in Liz would be tantalised beyond words by such a statement. She stopped, looked around and plonked herself down in her chair.

James nodded over at the door and a collective gasp of shock rippled through the audience as Ed and Arthur came in and took a seat either side of James.

Liz turned to Robert. "What the fuck is going on?"

James caught Christine's eye and she nodded.

"I turn thirty-three years old tomorrow and most of you think that's time I found myself a special someone." He put his hand on Ed's shoulder. "The fact is, I found that special someone twenty-eight years ago in a school yard not so far from here. Seven years ago, we realised we felt differently about each other."

Not a sound could be heard in the room. All eyes were focused on him.

"Then I threw it all away and do you know why? Because I was worried about how each and every one of you would react. I went for a quiet life instead of a decent one. I put your opinions above those of the man I love."

He turned and put his hand on Arthur's shoulder.

"Then, and how lucky is this, another wonderful man came into my life. And still I let your opinions stop me from being open to happiness. I let a group of…people try to force love out of my life for a second time. Well, today I raise a glass to my two special men and tell you all that there will be three kings at The King's Arms in future and anyone who doesn't like it can sup somewhere else."

Chapter Twenty

James sat, trembling. Outwardly, though, he looked like a rock. Ed couldn't remember loving him more than he did right at this moment. He caught Arthur's eye, who had also been staring at James with utmost admiration. No matter what happened after this, they were a team. Ed took in the sea of people staring at them. Faces he had known all his life. Faces that now knew who he'd been all his life.

Christine stood up first and started to clap. Rob and Jenny, who wiped a tear from her eye, closely followed, adding to the applause.

Then the whole place stood and clapped. James looked at him incredulously.

"I...I can't believe it."

Ed put his hand on his thigh. "People love you for who you are, James. Not what you are."

Even Mrs Turnbull had a tear. "Well, I always did like Graham Norton," she said to no one in particular.

But one person wasn't clapping. Liz had a face like a thunderstorm about to explode.

"Thank you, everyone," James said. "That's enough about us. It's nearly eight o'clock, so time for some drinks, I think. The bar is open."

The crowd didn't need telling twice and started to file out of the room.

Andrew came over to the table. "That was a very brave thing you did then, James."

"Thank you, Andrew. It means a lot." James blushed.

Christine dashed over. "I'm so proud of you," she said to James, leaning over the table and kissing him on the cheek.

"Nice work," Rob said. "Now come on, Mr Chair, you can't leave poor Becky to face this mob on her own."

James drained his wineglass. "Tell her I'll be five minutes, yeah?"

Rob turned to Ed and winked. "No problem."

Before long only James, Ed and Arthur remained in the dining room.

"Well, that went well."

Arthur kissed him on the cheek. "You're a bloody hero, that's what you are."

James turned to Ed and took his hand. "I should have done this years ago."

Arthur reached over and placed his hand on top of theirs. "No, you shouldn't. You'd never have let me in then."

James put his arm around Arthur and pulled him close. "You're right there." He wrapped his other arm around Ed.

"What have we here? Can't wait to maul at each other after you've shared your dirty little secret."

Ed and the other two spun around to see Liz standing in the doorway. Robert tried to stop her. "Come on, love. Leave it for tonight."

Liz got free from him and marched up to the table. "I'll leave nothing, thank you. How you could do that in this room makes me physically sick. This was our father's pub long before it was yours and God knows what he would make of this...filth."

Ed got up. "Liz—"

"Don't you dare. I blame you for this. Dragging our James into your ways."

"I wasn't dragged into anything. Don't be so ridiculous. I'm not talking to you when you're wound up," James said to her.

Liz leant forward, her face inches from James'. "You double-crossed me to get favour for your own disgusting little scheme. You snivelling little pervert. I won't forget this. You're dead to me."

She banged her hand on the table, making them all jump, before sweeping towards the door. When she got there, she turned around and scowled. "Don't think you'll be seeing the lads, either. I don't want my children around people like you. Do you hear me? Come near my family and I'll get the police onto you." She barged past Robert and out of the door.

Robert looked apologetically at them. "I'd better..."

"Run along, Robert," James said. "There's no point you getting into trouble, too."

Robert scuttled off after his wife.

As soon as they were alone, a huge sob escaped James. Ed rubbed his back and looked helplessly at Arthur. James managed to get his breathing under control and sat upright, wiping his eyes. "There's a shit ton of thirsty villagers out there. You two can make yourselves useful. We'll deal with this later."

Ed nodded. "Right you are, boss."

They followed him into the bar where an exasperated Becky shouted at the drinkers to form an orderly line.

James turned to Arthur and Ed. "Okay, Arthur, you're on glass collecting, and, Ed, you get the buggers washed and out to us." James pushed past Becky to his station behind the bar. "My, we are a rabid lot tonight. Mrs Turnbull, can I tempt you to a cheeky gin? It's a special occasion."

She giggled like a schoolgirl and turned to Christine. "Ooh, Mother's ruin! Why not?"

James had always been a natural people person. Ed had forgotten just how good a landlord he was.

"You didn't tell me we had a performer on our hands," Arthur said.

"Just wait until you really get to know him," Ed replied.

"I can't wait. But if you don't get these glasses washed, we'll be starting on a very bad footing."

Ed picked up the tray. "Aye, aye."

The next four hours passed in a blur. Ed could have sworn he'd washed the same glasses a hundred times as Arthur kept bringing more and more.

After a bumpy start, they soon settled into a rhythm with James and Becky keeping the till ringing.

By the time James rang last orders, most of the villagers were feeling no pain.

Rob stood on a stool. "At first I was afraid, I was petrified."

The whole pub launched into a rousing rendition of *I Will Survive*. Ed hoped bloody Liz could hear that all the way at her house.

Eventually James managed to wave off the last of the drinkers. Arthur and Ed sat on a banquette for a second, but Becky had taken over clearing glasses at warp speed. She kept banging them down on the bar before heading off for another load.

James frowned at Ed. "What's her problem?"

Ed shook his head. "Might as well find out tonight."

Becky came into the room and slammed a few more glasses on the bar.

"Do you mind? I'd like to have some left to serve with tomorrow if that's all the same to you."

She didn't stop to take in James' words. Instead, she picked up a cloth and started to vigorously wipe a table.

"Are you going to tell me what this is about?" James continued perplexed.

Becky had a face like thunder. "I'd like to know where this little revelation leaves me, that's what. It would have been nice if you'd told me I was out of a job before you announced it to the rest of the bloody village."

Ed got up. He could see that James about to lose his rag and didn't want any more drama in one night. He guided Becky down onto a stool and sat next to her. "Why would you be out of a job?"

Becky burst into tears. "Because he's got you two now. He won't be wanting me. You heard him. 'There'll be Three Kings at The King's Arms now'. He says my cooking is shit anyway."

James sat down opposite. "Becky, love, your cooking is shit, but I wouldn't be without you."

Ed scowled at him, but James couldn't stop giggling. "Becky, I'm working that farm single-handed and Arthur is going back to school next term. James has two new boyfriends, not two new slaves. You're still the apple of his eye, isn't she, James?"

James shook his head. "I don't know, you silly sod. Of course I want you to keep on working here. What would I do without you? If I didn't have your miserable face driving half the customers away, I'd be run off my feet."

Becky threw the rag at him. "I don't know what either of you see in that pig."

"That pig is going to tell you to clear off and get some sleep. My two new slaves can help me with the rest of this so it's ready for your inspection in the morning."

Becky glanced around. "I've done most of it, but fair enough. I'll see you tomorrow. Don't stay up late." She winked at Ed and walked out to the kitchen. At last the door slammed and all three breathed a sigh of relief.

"Fucking women," James said. "I thought by bedding down with two gorgeous men, I'd have a break from them."

"And Liz?" said Ed.

James kissed him on the forehead. "Liz will keep for another day. Tonight it's us three and I want us to seal the deal upstairs pretty soon so both of you get off your arses and get some glasses cleared up."

Ed and Arthur didn't need telling twice and flew around the pub as though their life depended on it.

The glasswasher started to make a peculiar noise as Ed put load after load through it.

James rested his hand on the beer pump. "You wouldn't think we'd spent the last two days in bed. You're like a man possessed."

Ed put his arms around James. "This is all I've ever wanted and more. To have you and him. I don't think I've ever been this happy in my life."

"Not even when you beat me at GCSE English?"

Ed thought for a second. That had been quite a victory. "Torn on that one."

"What did you get?" Arthur said, leaning on the other side of the bar.

"I got a B and he got a C," Ed told him triumphantly.

Arthur started to saunter away before looking over his shoulder at them. "A," he said.

James poked Ed in the ribs. "Oh dear, you've been owned."

Finally, the last glass was polished. The guest rooms were all full, so they shushed each other like naughty school children as they crept up the staircase.

"Avoid that step," Arthur told Ed.

He raised an eyebrow. "Oh, I see. I discovered that creaky step, I'll have you know."

Once they got into James' rooms, they stripped down to their boxers and climbed the ladder. Ed lay down on the bed as James and Arthur squeezed onto either side of him.

Suddenly a terrifying creak rang out.

"Fuck," James said. "The support. Quick, get down."

"I bloody told you this bed idea was stupid," Ed grumbled as he went back down the ladder.

"Calm down, Eduardo," Arthur said, following.

"Oh, for fuck's sake, James."

Arthur and James howled with laughter.

"Don't think you're going to be ganging up on the only decent cook in this outfit. It would be short-sighted."

Arthur gave him a big sloppy kiss. Suddenly, they both dodged out of the way as the duvet, pillows then mattress were upended over the top.

James got to the bottom of the ladder, panting. "Guess we'll have to get that reinforced."

Arthur snorted. "Imagine that titbit reaching Liz."

They made a bed in the middle of the lounge. All three climbed under the duvet, their bodies entwining as though they had been designed for that very purpose.

"I say we seal the deal tomorrow," Ed said. "You've knackered me out now."

Arthur snuggled into his side.

"You okay?" Ed asked, kissing his hair.

"Just thinking about school. Nothing about that is sorted, is it? You said I'll be going back, but not if there aren't any kids to teach."

James curled his body around Arthur's, letting his arm reach across and rest on Ed's thigh.

"That will be sorted by September, you mark my words. After that display downstairs, Liz won't dare go against the village. All those people are her customers, remember. Bloody hell, if she carries on, I'll set up a minibus service to the superstore in Holton."

Arthur reached for James' arm. "You're a good man, James Durkin. It's a shame she can't see that."

James sighed. "It's the lads I'm most upset about. I love those boys and not seeing them will be hard."

Ed turned on his side, so he faced Arthur and James. Liz had been so cruel using her children as a weapon against him. Even he had been surprised when she had fired that one. "You'll see them tomorrow. It's the fête, remember? Liz can hardly ban you. You're the king of Napthwaite."

James laughed on the other side of the bed. "And you two are my queens."

"I remember when my mum won first prize for her marrows," Ed said, thinking how happy she had been. "Dad was so proud. Mind you, we had to eat marrow for weeks. She had a lot of them before she could choose just the right one. I've never eaten it since."

The two men just looked at him, their eyes filling with tears. Ed realised what he had just done. It had felt right to speak about them with these two wonderful men.

James' hand found his and squeezed it.

"My dad was never much of a cook," Ed continued. "But that year Mum had summer flu and was stressing she wouldn't get the cupcakes done. He baked up a storm and came second. She wasn't happy, I can tell you. He never let her forget it either."

Arthur reached and put his hand over Ed's and James'.

That was how they all fell asleep.

Chapter Twenty-One

Ed heard movement inside. He knocked on the door again and finally Dean opened it.

"Uncle Ed."

He ignored the nerves jangling around his system. "Hi, Dean. Is your mum in?"

Joel came running into the hallway and straight into Ed, wrapping his small arms around his waist. "Uncle Ed, I haven't seen you in ages."

"Hi, kiddo. How are you?"

Joel looked very solemn. "It's the fête today and if I don't mither, I'm allowed two cakes from the stall."

"You'd best not mither then," Ed replied.

"Impossible mission," Dean said.

Liz appeared behind them with a face like thunder. "Dean, take your brother in the shop while I talk to Ed."

"I'm not working today," Dean complained.

"You are now. Move."

Muttering about fairness and family exploitation, Dean led Joel into the shop. Liz folded her arms at the door, an invitation inside obviously not forthcoming.

"Well?"

"You know what I'm here for. Come on, Liz, you can't do this to him. He's your brother. You're all he has."

Liz looked anywhere but at Ed. "He's made his choice."

She had always been hard-faced, but he couldn't remember when she had become this cruel.

"He hasn't made a choice. He's gay, Liz. Always has been and always will be. I should know."

Mrs Turnbull was putting her bins out across the gardens that lined the back of the houses. She seemed to be taking an inordinately long time to do it.

With a flick of her head, Liz gestured him inside and slammed the door on her nosy neighbour. "Go in the lounge. I don't want the boys hearing this."

She followed him in and shut the door. He sat on the sofa, upending a pile of folded washing.

Liz stood by the fireplace, scowling at him. "You listen to me. Just because that little shit has come into our village and poisoned both your minds, why should I let him do the same to me? What next? Dean? Joel?"

Ed sighed. "He hasn't poisoned anyone's minds. James and I were together for years. You know that now. He's gorgeous and never had a girlfriend. Didn't that seem odd to you?"

"Wrong. Stacey Allenby."

Ed couldn't help but laugh. "He snogged her on the French school trip and she dumped him because he wouldn't touch her tits."

Liz fiddled with her tabard, seemingly at a loss for what to say next.

"Liz," Ed said, leaning forward. "We've all had a bad time. Every one of us, including you. I know you're angry with him for the planning application and believe me, I knew nothing about that. But are you really angry that he's found happiness with someone you used to call a friend and someone who is probably the best teacher your son could ever have?"

Liz twisted her wedding ring. "But my dad —"

"Our parents are gone, Liz. We don't owe them anything but to be happy. Surely that's all you want for your kids, isn't it?"

She started to fill up. "It's been such a hard year. I don't know if I'm coming or going."

Ed leapt up and put his arm around her. "You need to stop and think instead of just rushing in. I will tell you now that I'll do the best I can to make James happy. So will Arthur. But we're not blood relatives. He loves those boys and you. That's why he lived a lie all his life. For you."

Liz had real tears in her eyes. "Are you saying he was miserable because of me? Is that it?"

"Yes I am." For a minute he thought he had penetrated the hard exterior but back it came.

"Or perhaps he was just vulnerable to you. Go on, bugger off. I'm sick of being told how to live my life."

Ed got up. "This is going to have further-reaching consequences than you realise. I really want you to remember I tried to help you." He didn't wait for another stream of insults but walked through into the shop. Dean and Joel were at the till.

"Uncle Ed —" Joel cried.

"I'm sorry, kiddo. I think it's best if I leave you to it." He couldn't bear to see the little boy's face fall like that, but he also didn't want to be chased out of there by his spiteful mother who he knew would soon be lurking amongst the tins of custard.

The green was a sea of people. The fête was in full swing. The usual stalls were doing a roaring trade. The coconut shy run by Matthew Johnstone had always been a favourite — Ed thought it wise to give that a wide berth this year. The penalty shootout seemed to be popular with James' number one fan, Andrew, in charge. Kids were flocking around that one.

Mrs Turnbull stood proudly behind the nearly new stall. Ed frowned at the figurine of E.T. and cassette of New Kids on the Block. *Nearly new in what century?*

"That's got all their hits on, you know," she announced. He dug in his pocket and handed over a five-pound note.

She rummaged in her polka-dot money belt.

"No, no, keep the change," he said, picking up the figurine and cassette.

"Oh goodness. I'll easily beat last year's takings at this rate."

"What did you make last year?"

"Five pounds, fifty pence." She beamed.

Before he could be hoodwinked into buying the set of coasters with pictures of dogs dressed as royalty, he made a beeline for the pub. Arthur stood outside, watching the proceedings. "Hey," Ed said.

"Hey yourself," Arthur replied, handing him his pint.

"Where's laughing boy?" Ed took a sip.

Arthur pointed into the centre of the open-sided marquee. Ed spluttered the lager at the sight of James being fed tiny slices of sponge cake by excitable elderly women. He whispered something to a man with a clipboard.

"The winner of the lightest sponge competition is Audrey Cleghorn."

A stout woman in perilously high heels did a little jig as her competitors retreated muttering to themselves. James waved and bounded over.

"You have cake crumbs all round your mouth," Ed said.

James rubbed his mouth. "It's not that I do this for pleasure, Eduardo. My responsibilities as chair of this parish's council are very wide ranging."

They wandered out into the crowd. A few people stared, but to Ed's relief, no one treated them any differently. He knew James would be analysing every reaction from people. No matter what his jolly exterior said.

His stomach dropped when he heard, "Uncle Ed. Uncle James… Mr Whittaker?"

Joel stood in front of them, very confused. Dean followed him with Liz hot on his heels.

Dean took a picture with his phone. "That's one for the photo album."

Liz barged past him, taking hold of Joel's hand. "Well done," she said to James.

Joel squirmed out of his mother's grasp and ran straight to Arthur, who knelt down to meet him.

"I thought you'd gone."

Arthur smiled. "I came back."

Joel's eyes widened. "Forever?"

Ed glanced at James whose eyes were filled with tears.

"Forever is a long time, but let's say I have no plans to leave." Arthur stared pointedly at Liz who had the decency to shift uncomfortably.

The little boy, overcome with emotion, flung his arms around Arthur's neck. "I've missed you more than I did my rabbit when he died."

Arthur returned the hug. "I've missed you too. All of you."

Joel pulled away. "Come on. Most of the others are at the penalty shootout. Please can you have a go?"

Arthur glanced at Liz. "Oh, I'm not sure…"

Liz shrugged. "Go on. You might as well."

He allowed himself to be dragged off by the little boy. The remaining four stood in awkward silence.

James broke the silence. "Come on, eldest. Let me whop your arse at the coconut shy. I've got ten minutes before I have to judge the most suggestive vegetable."

They wandered over to the shy. Suddenly Ed remembered who he had seen running it. This could be a bad idea. "James…"

Far too late.

Matthew Johnstone reared up to his full five-foot-eight when he saw their party approaching. "Ah, Chair," he said, frowning at James, then Ed. "And only one of his lovers. Don't tell me there's trouble in paradise already?"

Dean glanced from one to the other. "Lovers?"

Matthew put on a face of mock horror. "Oh dear, not let the family know yet?"

"You two?" Dean said.

Ed could see the penny dropping.

"And Mr Whittaker?"

Liz stepped forward. "That's enough of that. Thank you very much, Mr Johnstone. Come on, let's find your brother."

But Dean hadn't finished. "Well, that's one in your face, isn't it? You think you've got rid of one and he returns far more powerful, bringing two more with him, including your own brother."

The indignation on Liz's face made Ed want to burst into giggles, but James put his stern face on.

"That's your mother you're talking to, young man. Less of it."

Dean shocked everyone by hugging his mother. "Oh, Mother. You really are one in a million."

He sloped off, presumably to find some of his mates to share the news with.

Matthew Johnstone did not find this amusing though. His face looked as though the devil himself had descended from the church and demanded three tennis balls for a pound to win a coconut. "That child might think it funny, but I certainly do not."

Liz put her hand on his arm. "Matthew, listen to me…"

He leapt back from her touch. "Don't you dare lay your hand on me. You're all as bad as one another."

She reared up. "Meaning?"

"The same blood runs in your veins, too."

Liz planted her hands firmly on her hips. This meant trouble.

"And isn't it your blood that runs in your William's veins? The same William who got expelled from school for sucking off Alan Ramsay from Holton on the rugby pitch?"

A ripple of embarrassed laughter ran through the crowd. James stared at his sister in shock. Ed couldn't believe she had gone there. No one had mentioned that for nearly twenty years.

"William went to boarding school through mutual consent," Matthew roared. "He was not and is not a pervert like these two excuses for men."

James held his hands out. "Come on, Matthew. We've always got along. Calm down. There's no need for a scene."

Judging by the crowd that were amassing around them, they were a little late for that.

"You'd like that, wouldn't you? All the village coming running to your assistance. Can't fight your own battles. Isn't that typical of your sort?"

He stopped to draw breath and before he could launch into another tirade, he gripped his chest.

"Matthew!" James shouted, catching him as he fell like a dead weight.

"Oh, Jesus," Liz cried. "We need a first aider."

Ed had seen the St John's Ambulance on the other side of the green. A young lad ran to get them, but in the meantime a figure pushed through the crowd. It was Arthur.

"Get him on the floor," he barked. He fell onto his knees and reached for Matthew's wrist, clearly searching for a pulse. "Shit," he cried and started to perform CPR on the stricken man.

James started to try to push the crowd back. Liz and Ed joined him.

"Come on, folks, give him some room."

Begrudgingly people moved, parting when the St John's people arrived.

"I can't find a pulse," Arthur said.

The first one nodded and took over from him while the other hurriedly got a defibrillator out of its bag. They opened Matthew's shirt and attached the machine.

Ed hated being a gawker, but nothing could make him tear his eyes away. James stood next to him and reached for his hand.

"Clear," came the shout and Matthew's prone body convulsed.

They all looked at the ECG machine, and a cheer erupted as a blip appeared on the screen. Arthur seemed as though his legs were about to give way under him. James leapt forward and grabbed hold of him.

The St John's man stared up at Arthur. "Looks like you might have saved his life."

James turned to Ed. "Get him into The King's. I'll sort things out here."

Rob appeared at James' shoulder. "All of you go in. I'll fix this. I think you could do with a drink. Is there anyone who can go with him in the ambulance?"

A man appeared. He was model-looks handsome with blond sun-streaked hair and tan.

"I'll go."

"And you are?"

"I'm his gardener."

"Fine, come with me."

Ed and James ushered Arthur into the pub. As the sun had been beating down, it wasn't particularly busy inside, but Ed knew that would be about to change. "Let's go into the kitchen."

Becky looked aghast. "What the hell's happened now?"

"Don't ask. Just get us all a drink," James said. "That gin at the back."

"Oh, not that bloody gin," Arthur exclaimed.

They made it into the kitchen and all sank down at the table. Arthur put his head in his hands. "This fucking village will be the death of me, I swear it."

James and Ed tried to soothe him as they sat in silence for a second. Even Becky said nothing as she brought in their drinks.

"I'll be out in a bit, love," James said.

Arthur sat up and gratefully accepted the drink from Ed. "I never thought I'd have to do that. Bloody hell."

He took a healthy slug. The colour had started to return to his cheeks. Ed flung his arms around his shoulders and kissed him hard.

"I'm so proud of you," he said.

"Thanks," Arthur managed, slowly recovering from his shock.

James refilled Arthur's glass. "Tell you what. That gardener could see to my beds."

Arthur swatted him. "You already have the two best-looking men in the village. Greed is not an attractive quality."

"Sad, though, isn't it?" Ed said. "No one to go in the ambulance with you but a member of staff. Makes you think."

Before they could say anything else, a knock at the door rang through the room.

"Who the hell is that now?" James strode over. He let out a bit of a yelp at Liz standing on the back step.

Tears had streaked her makeup and she flung herself into her brother's arms. A shocked James froze for a second before wrapping his arms around her. Ed glanced at Arthur. This was a turn-up for the books.

"I'm so sorry, James," she said.

James guided her to the table and slid his drink over. She took a swig and caught Ed and Arthur staring at her.

"All of you. I've been a right bitch. I just got a bit carried away."

For once in his life, Ed had no idea what he wanted to do. Part of him wanted to send her away with a flea in her ear, but James needed family and Arthur needed peace. She could give them both. He sighed. "Liz, listen. You have been a bitch, I can't lie."

She had the decency to be a bit shocked.

"But we've all been on a hell of a rollercoaster these last few weeks. I can't speak for the other two, but I'm prepared to let bygones be bygones."

Liz sniffed and looked at Arthur.

"Seeing as I'm doing good today, I guess I'll go along with Ed," he replied.

Ed looked to James. He tried to read his face, but he stared at his sister before opening his arms to her.

"Of course, I forgive you, you rotten old cow. You're my sister."

This made her burst into tears again. She threw herself into James' arms as he hugged her. Ed felt a lump in his throat. He hadn't even dared dream for this moment. "I don't deserve it," Liz said, looking back at Ed and Arthur.

"No, you don't," they all said in unison.

Liz stared at them open-mouthed. "Fucking hell. You really are a package."

They all collapsed in fits of laughter.

Chapter Twenty-Two

Wrapping paper surrounded him. It had been a mad few days, but Arthur had rallied and clubbed together with Ed to get James an iPad, which he loved. They were naked and lazing in bed. Ed had already been out to tend to the animals and brought coffee to bed. James reached across to the bedside cabinet and pulled out a present that he and Ed solemnly presented to Arthur.

"What's this? It's not my birthday."

"Humour me," James said, putting his arm around Ed.

Arthur unwrapped a box. Something jangled inside. "What the hell?" He opened the box to reveal a bunch of keys on a heart-shaped keyring. "I don't understand."

"It's keys to The King's and this place," Ed said. "We know we can't invade Christine's, but we thought it might be nice for you to come and go as you please. They are your homes now."

Arthur launched forward, into their arms. They fell onto the pillows, laughing. But Arthur wanted more. He reached under the duvet and found both Ed and James' hardening cocks.

They scrambled out from under the duvet. James reached for Arthur and pulled him close, kissing him furiously while Ed reached across and ran his hands down Arthur's back.

Arthur detached from James and moved over to Ed, kissing him and reaching for his cock. James had got there first and sucked hard, causing Ed to moan.

Arthur straddled Ed's chest. James ran his tongue up Ed's cock and onto Arthur's hole inches away. He licked hard, alternating between the two. Both men were moaning into their kiss, which made his own cock pulse. James sat on his heels, just watching these two gorgeous men who were his. This was the best birthday he could ever remember.

Straddling Ed's waist, he moulded his chest against Arthur's back, who leant into it, letting James run his hands down his body and to his cock.

James had never realised being with two other men gave such freedom. The possibilities were endless. He saw the hunger in Ed's eyes as he lay on the pillow, watching him and Arthur enjoying themselves, straddling him.

"Get me a condom," James whispered into Arthur's ear.

He dutifully reached across and got one from the rapidly diminishing packet on the side and handed it to him with the lube.

James moved down the bed and rolled it onto Ed's cock. He ran the lube onto his own arse and gingerly lowered himself down onto Ed's throbbing dick.

James very rarely bottomed but something about these two made him want everything.

"Oh God, yes," Ed said.

Ed locked eyes with James, who gingerly lowered himself on his hard cock. It took him a second to get used to Ed inside him before he began to move up and down.

Ed pawed at James' cock. James pushed his hand away. He would come in seconds if he carried that on. "Not right now," he said with a wink.

Instead, Ed turned and started to suck at Arthur's cock. James felt incredible as he picked up speed and rode Ed hard.

The bed shook violently as the men bucked and rocked their way towards the peak.

"I'm going to come," Ed panted, ignoring James' pleas and pulling hard at his cock. Ed cried out as the orgasm ripped through him just as James' followed, filling Ed's hand. Arthur also let out a yell, gripping James' shoulder as he came.

They collapsed onto the bed and into one another's arms.

"Jesus Christ," James panted. "If it stays as good as that, we might as well get rid of the TV."

Arthur moved over onto his side, resting his head on Ed's still-heaving chest.

"Poor old lad. Do we have to go steady on you for your birthday?"

James swatted him gently. "Less of the old."

Arthur spun around to get up off the bed. "I suppose we'll have to conserve your energy. We've got all day after all."

James stood up too. "No we don't. We have lunch, remember."

"Do we have to?" Ed said, clearly refusing to move.

"Oh, we have to, Eduardo."

Ed grabbed him and play wrestled him onto the bed before straddling him. "Today is your birthday, so I'm letting you have that. After today, end of."

Arthur came over and tickled Ed. "Oh, Eduardo. What you gonna do about it?"

They both fell on top of James.

It took them about an hour to get ready. It didn't help that they ended up having an incredibly steamy shower together which meant they were late.

"This is your bloody fault," Arthur panted as they trotted down the farm track.

"I can't help being irresistible to the pair of you," James replied.

They made it into the village in record time and soon found themselves knocking at the door. Dean flung it open.

"Uncle James, Uncle Ed and…Uncle Arthur?"

"Just Arthur will do fine." Arthur smiled.

Dean led them in. James couldn't believe it. The place was spotless. Not a pile of books or anoraks or paperwork in sight. "Bloody hell," he exclaimed. "I hope you can get to your beds tonight. Your rooms must be full."

Liz, feverishly checking her pots and pans, stuck two fingers up at him. "Less of your lip, thank you." She came across and gave him a kiss on the cheek. "Happy birthday."

The smell made his mouth water. She was doing a roast and if she had learnt one thing from their mother, it was cooking.

"Go on through." She ushered them. "Dean, get them a drink. Beer...or perhaps wine is more for you."

Ed and Arthur followed Dean, but James hung back. "Thank you for doing this, sis. It's quite the turnaround. You wanted us all tarred and feathered a day ago."

Liz swatted him with a tea towel. "I will take this mocking for precisely one week, so make the most of it, James Durkin." She stroked his cheek. "I'm not going to pretend that it's not difficult for me, but what I've seen, really seen, has made me think. I only want you to be happy."

He took her hand and kissed it. "And an extension to the shop wouldn't go amiss," he said with a wink.

She grabbed her hand away and flicked his ear. "Now that little issue isn't over, you double-crossing little shit. Go on with you."

He went through to the dining room where Joel had commandeered Arthur to demonstrate his latest game on some handheld device. Robert, Ed and Dean were deep in conversation about the latest real ale from a brewery in Stockley Bridge.

"Here he is," Robert said, handing him a glass. "Get your gob around that. You should have this in the pub."

He tasted the beer. It wasn't bad.

Sitting down at the table, he declared, "Before I change the bar, I'm getting a new chef."

"Thank God for that," said everyone in unison.

Liz came in and perched on a chair at the head of the table. "Fifteen minutes."

Robert handed her a glass of wine, which she took a hearty swig from. James noticed her hand shaking.

He couldn't remember seeing her so nervous. It touched him. Even after all the nastiness, she did care.

Dean, Ed and Robert took their seats. It felt nice to be all around a table together and almost incredible to James. It had been a crazy year, but if this was the payoff, then it had all been worth it.

"Oh, that reminds me," Liz said, leaping up. She gingerly opened the door to the cupboard under the stairs.

James spied an Aladdin's cave of things piled up inside. "Steady, Liz. You're going to be buried."

"Piss off," came the muffled reply.

She emerged, triumphantly holding a carrier bag. She delved inside and produced a gift in bright pink wrapping paper. James frowned when it went to Ed.

"For me? But it's James' birthday."

Liz cleared her throat and glanced uncomfortably around. "It's a 'sorry for being a bitch' present."

Ed looked lost for words. "Thank you, Liz. It's really not necessary."

"Just open it." Arthur laughed.

Ed ripped the paper off and revealed a *Wizard of Oz* DVD. James only just managed to keep his giggles at bay as Ed put on his best fake smile. "Oh that's...wonderful. Thank you."

Liz fiddled with her hands. "I know it's popular." She drew another gift out of the bag and handed it to Arthur who took it with a little trepidation.

"Thank you." He ripped off the paper to reveal an illuminous pair of rainbow socks.

"Wow, these are...bright. They will be great for playground duty in the winter, won't they, Joel?"

Joel had been allowed cherryade so there was no noise coming from him. James knew that wouldn't be the case in a couple of hours' time. He intended to be beating a hasty retreat by then.

Liz scrunched the plastic bag up and put it in the pocket of her tabard. "Dean, go on," she said, nodding her head to the door.

Dean jumped up and returned with a big present in the same paper. He proudly handed it to James.

"Thanks, squirt."

He ripped the paper off to reveal a large picture frame. In the middle lay the word *FAMILY* and around it were pictures of him with the boys, Liz and Robert, their parents and at the bottom the picture taken of him, Ed and Arthur at the fête.

The tears welled up inside him and he didn't even try to stop them. He looked around the table at the faces that he loved the most in the world, despite what they had been through and probably would go through in the future.

Right now, at this moment, life was perfect, and he would do his absolute best to keep things that way.

Want to see more from this author? Here's a taster for you to enjoy!

Village Affairs: Three's Company
Kristian Parker

Excerpt

Steam swirled in the air as Will Johnstone took the lid off the bone marrow broth that had sold like proverbial hotcakes since he'd insisted it went on the menu.

"Smells delicious," Stacey, the new waitress, said with a wink.

Will smiled weakly. She had been flirting with him ever since she'd started. He would have to get one of the waiters to fill the poor girl in. She didn't stand a chance.

To the untrained eye, the kitchen seemed to be in total pandemonium, but Will understood every move of this dance. He should. He'd been sous chef at Haven in Shoreditch for three years.

Serving under renowned chef, Anton Romano, he'd learnt all the foibles that his cantankerous boss preferred. As usual, Anton patrolled the pass where the plated meals waited to be served. If they stayed there longer than three minutes, he would scream at the restaurant staff until he went hoarse.

The month of August meant the traditional lull while valued customers enjoyed time on the beach in some far-flung place. Haven had that reassuringly expensive air that meant the clientele was more London's high society rather than tourists. Will had decided to use this time to test out new dishes before the inevitable surge in September that built steadily to Christmas.

"Are you going to let all the air get to that fucking broth?" Anton shouted across the room. Will realised Anton meant him and dropped the lid with a clatter.

He didn't even bother replying. Anton would be on to something else by now. That appeared to be the mousy new waitress whom he seemed determined to drive out of the door in less than two days. Will couldn't remember if that would be a personal best for Anton or not.

These days, he didn't even bother getting to know the wait staff unless Gustav, the maître d', tipped him off that they'd lasted the first month. They would tend to stay on then.

Will hated kitchens in August. The heat outside made it unbearable. He'd often tried to persuade Anton to reduce the number of hot dishes they served but Anton wouldn't have any of it. He didn't seem to feel the heat or the cold.

The intensity of the kitchen had started to lessen, the orders coming in slower. Anton stalked past him towards his office.

"Anton, could I have a—?" Will started.

"You may not," came the reply.

The staff regarded Will with amusement. They loved it when Anton treated him like shit. Anton liked to play a divide-and-rule game in his kitchen. He ruled with a culture where he positively encouraged climbing on top of colleagues, and at least three people were eyeing Will's position.

The smell of the duck main being prepped at the next station filled Will's nostrils. Anton might be a bastard, but he was an absolute genius too.

It had gone eleven and there would be no more orders. His body ached, but he had that adrenalin rush he loved after a mad shift. It would be hours before he could even think about sleep. As the staff scrubbed everything in sight, he made his way through to the office.

Anton sat with his feet up on the desk, engrossed in a recipe book that could have dated to Noah's time on the ark.

"That looks interesting," Will said. Ever the optimist, he could almost imagine one day the ice thawing, and Anton bothering about their working relationship.

Anton snapped the book shut with a bang and put it in his drawer. He scowled at Will, daring him to speak. Tonight clearly would not be that night.

As a concession to his seniority, Will had the honour of being able to hang his coat and bag up in Anton's office rather than the changing area. Instead of engaging with a riled Anton, he chose retreat.

He could visualise the cold bottle of Sancerre in the fridge at home if bloody Angela hadn't stolen it.

"This came for you," Anton said.

Putting his jacket on, Will turned around to see Anton holding up a letter. Will frowned. *Who sends letters these days?*

"It's from head office," Anton continued. His expression suggested he was passing something toxic to Will.

Head office was Anton's kryptonite. People only mentioned it if they absolutely had to. Anton had this fantasy that Haven was his own personal restaurant.

He didn't want to accept that they were really being bankrolled by a Chinese investment firm. Most of the communications with head office were done by Will. It was nice to know he came in useful for the boring stuff.

"Weird they didn't just email," Will replied.

Anton stood and wandered to the drinks cupboard they had in the office, that Will had been warned on pain of death to never touch.

"Fancy a whisky before you go?" Anton said, trying to come across as friendly which really did not suit him.

Will could have been knocked down with a feather. "Erm…fine. Just a small one."

He poured a generous slug of Will's favourite, Hibiki. His mouth started to come alive in anticipation.

Anton raised his glass. "To Haven."

"Haven," Will replied.

He took a sip. His tastebuds exploded with all the different flavours of honey, orange, sandal and oak. They fought and danced together as he took a second to enjoy it.

"Good stuff," Anton said, smacking his lips.

"Amazing. My absolute favourite."

"A man of taste," Anton said, walking to his chair and sitting. He gestured to the chair in front of the desk.

Will lowered himself and waited. This Hibiki had more strings attached to it than a double bass.

"It seems one of the little shitcans out there has made a complaint," Anton said.

Everything slotted into place now. Anton didn't want to lose face in the kitchen but didn't mind trying to curry favour behind closed doors. *What a wily bastard.*

Anton pushed the bottle to his side of the desk. Will sank in his seat with a feeling of gloom coming over him. This was going to be a long session.

* * * *

An hour later and an exhausted Will let himself into his apartment, the remains of the bottle of whisky gurgling around in his backpack and his ears still ringing from Anton's rant.

Angela lay on the sofa with the TV blaring out a repeat of a soap opera. She opened her eyes as he put his bag down. "What time is it?" she said, stretching.

"Just gone two."

She frowned. "You're late."

"Ugh. Anton needed a friend."

"I thought he hated you."

Will stared out of the floor-to-ceiling windows at the view of Canary Wharf. He had to take three Tubes to get to work but he'd bought this place when he'd got his first professional job and wouldn't give it up for anything.

"One of the waitresses has made a complaint. I'm getting dragged into it. Lucky me."

Angela sat up and leant across to retrieve her half-drunk glass of wine. "And he wants you to defend his honour I suppose," she replied, taking a sip.

Will couldn't even be bothered to get a glass for himself, instead just holding his hand out. Angela gave him the glass, still staring at him.

"Got it in one." He took a sip. "Hey that's my bloody Sancerre."

Angela crawled across the velvet couch to his end and snuggled up to him.

"You're the best friend a girl could wish for."

"And you're a bloody thief."

"But you love me."

Will gently swatted her on the head. "Just as well, isn't it?"

Angela had been a waitress at Haven when he'd first started. It hadn't taken long until someone had seen her potential and she'd soon made a name for herself in the world of PR. He'd tried to get her to help the restaurant, but she despised Anton and refused to put her name to making him a success.

"It was only a matter of time before someone took that wanker on," she said, yawning.

He couldn't even argue. Anton played a dangerous game with his sexist comments. Will didn't know if he would cover Anton's arse yet again or gamble by telling the truth.

Whatever happened, it would have to wait for another time.

"How was your day?" he asked as he drained the glass. Sometimes he forgot about the world outside Haven.

"Oh, you know, went to the gym, had a few meetings, applied for a job in New York."

"Whoa, what?"

"Relax. I won't get it. They want someone to run a massive campaign for a baking show over there. Everyone is going for it. I've got no chance."

He thought about life without her. It didn't seem very appealing. He extracted himself from Angela and stood.

"I'm having a shower then bed. I'm knackered."

"You know, if you came out from behind those bloody cookers once in a while, bed might be a more exciting option."

Not this again. He walked over to his bedroom door. "Change the record before the morning, please. Good night."

As he closed the door, she shouted, "Your penis is begging to be released, William Johnstone."

He stripped down and threw his uniform in a heap in the corner, catching sight of himself in the mirror. At thirty-five years old, he still had his looks. The six-pack he'd crafted so diligently in his twenties might have disappeared, but he didn't brush up too badly.

He tried to remember the last time he'd had sex. *Ah yes. Brian.* The guy from the gym. He frowned — that had been his birthday treat to himself. His birthday was in April. It was now August.

Perhaps Angela had a point.

Another task for tomorrow then.

About the Author

I have written for as long as I could write. In fact, before, when I would dictate to my auntie. I love to read, and I love to create worlds and characters.

I live in the English countryside. When I'm not writing, I like to get out there and think through the next scenario I'm going to throw my characters into.

Inspiration can be found anywhere, on a train, in a restaurant or in an office. I am always in search of the next character to find love in one of my stories. In a world of apps and online dating, it is important to remember love can be found when you least expect it.

Kristian loves to hear from readers. You can find his contact information, website details and author profile page at https://www.pride-publishing.com

PRI))E

Sign up for our newsletter and find out about all our romance book releases, eBook sales and promotions, sneak peeks and FREE romance books!

Printed in Great Britain
by Amazon